The Surrender

and Other Stories

Mabel Segun

Longman Group Limited,
Longman House, Burnt Mill, Harlow,
Essex CM20 2JE, England
and Associated Companies throughout the world

Longman Publishing Group
10 Bank Street
White Plains
New York 106001-1951
USA

Copp Clark Longman Ltd
2775 Matheson Blvd East
Mississauga
Ontario L4W 4P7
Canada

© Longman Group Limited 1995

All rights reserved. No part of this publication may be reproduced, stored in a retrieval system, or transmitted in any form or by any means, electronic, mechanical, photocopying, recording, or otherwise, without the prior written permission of the Publishers.

First published 1995

British Library Cataloguing in Publication Data
A CIP record is available for this title

Series Editor
Stewart Brown

Set in 11 on 12pt Baskerville

Produced through Longman Malaysia, PP

ISBN 0 582 25833 2

Dedicated to

Omowunmi,

my favourite daughter who also happens to be my only daughter

Introduction

The fifteen stories in this collection were written over a period of forty years: 1953–93. They have been selected for their common theme – the relationship between men and women which, in the context of Nigeria where they are set, is often influenced by cultural considerations. The Nigerian societies in which these stories take place are male-oriented societies where women are generally regarded as appendages to men, if not their outright properties. The survival of a marriage, or its success, is usually based on the woman's ability to bear children, preferably male, and people attain immortality only when they are outlived and buried by their children with appropriate prescribed traditional ceremonies. They are also societies which hold female chastity and marital fidelity in high esteem while permitting a man to practise legal polygamy, indulge openly in extra-marital affairs or even commit bigamy by taking advantage of the three marriage systems established in the country; viz., western-style marriage by ordinance, traditional marriage and muslim marriage rites. Although in law marriage by ordinance outlaws any other form of marriage, women never evoke this law against their erring husbands as this is culturally taboo.

Taboos and belief in witchcraft, oracles and traditional medicine are also portrayed in some of the stories as influences over women, either as victims or desperate suppliants who resort to traditional remedies whenever they encounter culturally aggravated problems such as barrenness and the *abiku* syndrome, *abiku* being the Yoruba word for a child who keeps on dying and being reincarnated again and again in the same woman.

Since these stories were written over such a long period the reader may wonder if they are still applicable to present-day Nigeria, considering the influence which Western education and Christianity wielded in colonial days before Nigeria gained independence in 1960. These two tools of cultural imperialism did indeed denigrate the culture of the country but it was only partially suppressed and the search for cultural identity after independence has rehabilitated the old religions and beliefs which many people now practise along with foreign religions such as Christianity and Islam. Thus in Nigeria the traditional and the modern exist side by side. However, the power of taboos and other socio-cultural regulations has been eroded by urbanization, the breakdown of the extended family system and the dictates of modern living. Women are now hardly ever required to produce evidence of their chastity on their wedding night as portrayed in *The Feast* and female undergraduates now enjoy considerably greater social freedom than they have in *The Surrender*, a story in which tradition-oriented male undergraduates clamour against the college authorities whom they regard as agents of imperialism while at the same time denying female undergraduates the right to freedom of association and expression. Written seven years before independence in 1960, the story gives an insight into the vibrant nationalism of the time as well as student life in the first Nigerian university, then called University College, Ibadan, where there were fourteen female students to about five hundred male students, a proportion which made the women more visible and therefore ready objects of vilification. The story won the 1954 Nigerian National Festival of the Arts Literature Prize.

Three stories are set during the civil war of 1967–70 when the Ibos of the eastern part of the country tried to secede from the federation and set up the republic of Biafra. The war was precipitated by the massacre of the Ibos resident in the north of the country following a coup d'etat in 1966, the first of many. It brought into political prominence military men such as General Ehi in the story of that title. The other two stories, *The Vitamins* and *Man of the House* reveal a new development in the relationship between men and women – a relationship in which women seem to have gained a new confidence in themselves. It is not surprising therefore to find the Nigerian male becoming more subtle in his assertion of male authority as in *A Child is a Child*, one of the most recent stories.

Nigerian women enjoy equal pay with men and large numbers wield economic power, especially market women. They are still far from gaining political and socio-cultural equality. Hopefully with time the discriminating practices will become extinct.

Mabel Segun

Author's acknowledgements

The Sunday Times, Lagos, for 'By the Silent Stream' and 'Terror of the Curse' (published as 'Terror of the Hoodoo'); *Modern Woman*, Lagos, for 'Bola'; *Nigeria Magazine*, Lagos, for 'The Feast' and 'The Confidante' and Horst Erdman Verlag, Tubingen in *Nigerian Writing* by Momodu, A. and Schild, U., eds, 1976 for 'Bola'.

Contents

Introduction

Title of Stories	Date written	Page
The Surrender	1953	1
Bola	1964	17
The Feast (*an earlier version was written in 1956*)	1991	27
Man of the House	1992	39
A Child is a Child	1992	45
The Vitamins	1992	57
The One Who Came Back	1957	63
By the Silent Stream	1957	69
General Ehi	1986	75
The Mat	1959	85
'Who Will Bury Me?'	1959	91
Ahimie's Wives	1993	99
The Confidante	1964	101
Terror of the Curse (*originally 'Terror of the Hoodoo'*)	1957	109
The Voice by the Lagoon (*an earlier version entitled 'The Voice by the River' was written in 1977*)	1993	115
Glossary		128

The Surrender

Oh, she's dying! Run for the doctor, someone! She will die! Wake up, Keke! It's me – Funke. She's dead! Sobs and hysterics. Confused noise. Keke heard it all in a haze. She was glad she was dead. At last! What a relief! The noise was rising. It sounded like the noise of a fast flowing river. What was that river in the Underworld? The Styx? Oh, it was the Styx. Nice, kindly Styx bearing her dead body away. But it looked white. It should be black, should it not? Keke was not sure.

'Oh, Keke, why did you do it?'

She mumbled, 'I didn't.'

They walked her up and down, up and down. She was so tired. The Styx. So tired, swimming, swimming. So cold too.

After some time she saw dimly the whitewashed walls, the blurred outline of faces. Funny, they seemed to be swimming – indistinct. Sounds of hysterical laughter. Oh, she's opened her eyes. She's not dead. Not dead. Keke's mind tried to grasp the meaning. No, she disagreed, she was dead; only her ghost was moving – her restless spirit, restless even in death.

The doctor and the warden of the Women's Hall came in.

'How long have you been walking her?' the doctor asked. 'Half an hour? Good. Let her rest.'

They placed her back in bed. The doctor felt her pulse.

'Not too slow. She'll be all right soon. How many did she take? Six? Not very dangerous.'

The warden said, 'We'll have to hush it up.'

'Of course,' the doctor agreed.

They took her to hospital. To rest, the doctor said. She felt so tired. Why didn't they let her sleep on? She was so tired. Every quarter of an hour the nurse woke her up. She kept on mumbling sleepily. 'Sleep, want sleep.'

By the following morning she was fully awake. She had been put in a side ward, so she was by herself she noted with relief, but the room looked so bare, so cold, like the Styx. She was feeling bitter but was too depressed to think about it. The nurse came in briskly, smiled at her and said, 'How are we this morning?' She took her temperature and pulse and went out. Soon the other girls came to see her. 'Oh, we're so happy. How you frightened us! Whatever made you do it?'

You'd like to know, wouldn't you, and gloat over it? No, thanks. She turned her face to the wall.

When she opened her eyes, she found the warden sitting on the chair by her bed.

'You are all right now,' she said. 'The doctor came when you were asleep. Put on your things and we'll go back to the college.'

She was silent as they drove to the college though the warden kept up a continual monologue. As they entered the college, she could see some students craning their necks to see her properly. She leant further back into the corner.

In the evening the warden came and found her alone and crying.

'Now, we mustn't give way like this, must we?' the warden said. 'Come along; there's a small party in my place. It will cheer you up no end.'

'I don't want to …'

'No, no, no. Oh, there you are, John. She won't come.'

'Tch, tch, tch,' said John. 'She must, of course. Professor's orders, you know.'

He pulled her to her feet and he and his wife took her to their house. On the way the warden said to her husband, 'Did you know you were breaking college rules by entering the room of a female undergraduate? You ought to know better at your age.'

'Now, Mrs Mann, don't you be rude,' her husband replied.

'For my benefit,' Keke's mind registered mechanically. She walked between them as they teased each other and laughed rather more than usual.

'Hello, hello, everybody. I've brought Miss Ojeru along. We're going to play musical chairs. Bring the chairs here.'

There was a stampede for the tall dining chairs.

'How tactful of him,' Keke thought.

They played musical chairs for some time. She was soon out as she made no attempt to struggle for a chair. She sat in a corner of the room and watched the others. Soon the professor's son came to join her.

'Hello, I haven't shown you my sports album, have I? I'll go and fetch it.'

She spent the rest of the evening looking through the album.

The affair was hushed up, thanks to the reticence of the doctor and the warden. There were speculations of course, but these hardly touched her. The official story was that she had accidentally taken an overdose of a sleeping drug, but some people shook their heads and looked knowingly at one another.

One morning the warden summoned her to her office. When she arrived the warden was not there. She sat on the edge of a chair, looking tense. As the warden entered, she jumped up nervously.

'Do sit down, Keke. I'm sorry I'm late. I had to see Dr Welles.' She made some tea and handed Keke a cup.

'Keke, why didn't you come to me when things were going so badly with you?'

'I just didn't think of it. I was so used to being without friends.'

'But I thought you had many friends. You were always so sociable and cheerful.'

'They weren't real friends. I wasn't going to let them know I was unhappy. They'd gloat over it.'

'Poor you. That was the trouble. It's bottling it up that causes half the trouble. Well, let's not think of the past. Let's talk about the future. I know it's going to be difficult for you to forget what has happened, but do try to.'

'I can't,' Keke said.

'Promise me you'll make an effort.' Keke nodded.

'Good. Well, about the future – I know you're very bitter

now. You're in a very difficult position. You're trying to break out of a sort of purdah and the men don't approve.'

'Nor do the women, either, for that matter,' Keke said bitterly.

'Don't be so bitter.'

'It's true. They hate me even more than some of the men do.'

'The word "hate" is too strong. I would rather say they resent you. The position of women in this country is delicate. They dislike the purdah-like restriction as much as you do and they resent you for having the courage to break out of it. They want the joy of freedom without its cost. Well, the most important thing is for you to recognize the inevitable difficulties. All suffragettes have to suffer. They did in England. Once you reconcile yourself to the difficulties, your sense of humour will help you along. That is all. If you have any more problems, don't hesitate to come to me.'

'Thank you,' said Keke.

She was leaving when the warden called her back.

'I've forgotten the most important thing. The *Scorpion* has been banned. You won't have any more trouble from that quarter.'

As Keke walked towards her hostel she heard an uproar coming from the Students' Union Building. When she got near it she heard someone shout, 'We won't have it! We won't have it! The authorities have no right to interfere with our newspaper. They're trying to muzzle the Union!'

A male student shouted, 'We must stage a demonstration. This is another display of imperialism. We must fight for our freedom.'

Keke passed on. She was accustomed to hearing such phrases. Freedom to do what? To oppress others?

But the students did not stage a demonstration. They usually said things they never had any intention of putting into practice. Instead a few cool-headed ones among them interviewed the Principal.

'We cannot allow this sort of thing to go on,' said the

Principal. 'You have repeatedly been warned but you don't appear to have benefited from the warnings.'

The President of the Union said, 'This time we promise there will be no more scandalous publications in the *Scorpion*.'

So the paper started publishing again and for a time steered clear of scandal. Soon the students began to complain that the paper was extremely uninteresting and sales dropped. The *Scorpion* was not doing its work of stinging. The publication committee was torn between fear of inevitable bankruptcy and the bold step of publishing and being damned. They chose the latter. This time the victim was another girl and it was an unfortunate thing for the publication committee that she belonged to the most vocal ethnic group in the college. Keke was coming back from lectures when she saw a gathering of students. They all belonged to the ethnic group. They were shouting, 'Our women have been insulted! Our people have been insulted. We won't tolerate it!'

The next moment the gathering dispersed. Keke was still wondering what was happening when they came back armed with axes and matchetes. They made for the office of the *Scorpion* and hacked the door to pieces. They brought out the unsold copies and the files, and made a bonfire of them on the lawn. After that they moved towards the rooms of the editor and the secretary. What massacre would have occurred once the flimsy doors yielded under the assault was prevented by the arrival of the Principal, who had been hastily summoned by a college porter.

And this time the *Scorpion* was banned for good.

But Keke was very bitter, even as she was sitting in the dining hall she was thinking about her predicament. There had been no ethnic demonstration over her own more damaging scandal. She saw the futility of belonging to a minority ethnic group in a community where ethnicity was the basis for every action, every decision. Sometimes it was superimposed by that type of nationalism that saw imperialism in every action of the college authorities.

Keke hated everybody. Sometimes she would clench her

fists but she knew she would never hit anybody. People were near enough to hurt you, but too remote to be hurt by you. They believed in freedom for everybody and wallowed in nostalgic references to the good old days of the Black Man's integrity. They also believed in the ultimate demonstration of the superiority of the Black Race over every other. But they did nothing about it. Oh, how they talked about it, in the dining-hall, in the commonroom, on the sports field, at political meetings, even outside the chapel. How they rolled out the words – smooth, empty phrases that rang out so hollowly they made one think of those African musical resonators decked with shells – empty shells. One day, in a speech against imperialism, one of them said:

'I am a lover of freedom, freedom for everybody, be he a prince, a pauper, a ...'

The catalogue rolled on wearisomely until the chairman banged on the table. Keke was tempted to shout, 'Charity begins at home! Emancipate your women first!'

Doubtless the assembly would be electrified, shocked out of their smugness, but almost immediately they would recover. Oh, cold, demoniacal fury! Crucify her!

Someone nudged her; she looked up to see a male student at the table scowling in impotent annoyance.

'Oh, the pepper, did you say? So sorry.'

And she passed down the pepper. 'The pepper' sounded like 'crucify her' when you weren't listening. Looking at the scowling young man, she almost laughed. He had been torn between stretching for the chilli pot and doing without the spice he loved so much. The dilemma had seemed so momentous to him – ridiculously momentous. Well-bred young men with western education never stretched for anything at table but they could publish newspapers full of filthy, scandalous lies.

It is wonderful the way one hears one's name even in the market.

'You know the truth about Keke's illness, don't you?'

'Who wouldn't? I wasn't born yesterday, you know.'

'The strange question is,' continued the first voice slowly, quoting the scriptures like the proverbial Devil, 'whether it is easier to forsake the sinner's path or to commit suicide?'

'The latter, obviously,' replied the second voice and they both laughed.

Keke left the table abruptly, spilling the contents of the water jug. The still annoyed young man made a sound of disgust.

Her mind running on cats, especially jealous cats, Keke walked along the laterite road running round the College. Head down, she began idly to count the number of white stones bordering the road. At the corner of a building she came into sharp collision with a male student. Adebayo was a member of the athletics club and that was where they had first met. He said, 'Heavens! You turned philosopher, or do they look up into the sky? I forget which. Anyway, ordinary human beings look where they are going.'

'I'm no ordinary human being.'

'Nonsense. You're too conceited, that's what's the matter with you. Where are you going, by the way?'

'To the bookshop. To browse. I've no money. I get my allowance next week.'

'Just like you to go mooning around. Have you been to the reservoir?'

'No.'

'Let's go there. It's so enchanting. You can see the sun set beautifully there.'

She looked at him in wonder.

'I thought Nigerians never notice the sunset. Only crazy people like me do.'

'Don't be so hard on yourself,' Adebayo replied.

They walked on. She was half conscious of curious glances. Another one of them, they seemed to say. Well, she was beyond them now. They could only make her bitter, and after some time bitterness becomes so sweet. From a corner of the sports field they could see the water reservoir.

'Come, I'll race you to the top,' Adebayo said.

Adebayo reached the top first – but only just.

'I forgot you were in training,' he said. 'How many laps did you run this morning?'

'Eight.'

'That's two miles. Are you really aiming at the Championships or …'

'Nothing so elevated. It's just to keep me fit.'

He looked at her and added, 'and trim. Has anyone ever told you you've got the best figure in this place?'

'No one, thank you, and I don't like flattery.' Her tone was cold.

'I wasn't flattering you, but if you don't like it, I'm sorry.'

From then on they sat silently side by side. From the reservoir they could see the greater part of the town. The setting sun lit up the area to their right and made the red mud buildings look even redder. The town lacked planning. It was hilly and each house nestled crookedly against the other as if for protection. Immediately below them was the college, a makeshift wooden affair, housed in a former army field barracks.

'I often spend many an evening here trying to make out the different college buildings. They're so alike, aren't they?' Adebayo said.

'Like the people in them,' Keke replied.

Adebayo felt that he understood her feelings, so he kept quiet. They went back to gazing over the town. The hills that surrounded it were no longer as green as they were. From one of them rose a big tower, small in the distance, Bower Tower, named after a colonial officer.

Suddenly Keke said, 'Why do you like me? I thought everybody here hated me.'

Startled, Adebayo looked at her.

'That is the mistake you make. Of course nobody is ever liked by everybody, but I can assure you you are the most popular girl here.'

'Really! And the Christian idea is to destroy what you like, like kiddies tearing their favourite dolls to pieces. I think I understand the psychology. Very human. I'll write a thesis on it.'

The Surrender

'You needn't be so bitter, you know, though I must say you look ravishing when you're sad. Oh, sorry, no compliments, I forgot. Well, the situation is this. I don't like preaching but you are such a stubborn pessimist that I've got to do it. Er ... er,' he paused, thinking, then continued, 'have you heard of sour grapes?'

'Uhhuh?'

'That is half the trouble. Half the male students would like to be your boyfriend. Honestly. The other half is caused by our narrow outlook. Those who genuinely dislike you are conservatives who have not yet got used to the idea of a woman mixing freely with men, joining all the clubs, doing sports ... We can't help it now. Maybe we will some day.' He paused, then said, 'Why don't you conform if it makes you so unhappy?'

'I should be unhappier still,' Keke said, 'I love joining clubs and I love sports. Why should I hide away just because I am female?' Adebayo said nothing and for sometime there was silence between them.

At last she got up.

'Come, let's go. I'm sorry I've been such bad company. I enjoyed the view, though. Thank you.'

They went down the steep side of the reservoir.

They began to visit the water reservoir frequently. One day, Adebayo said, 'You know I love you, don't you?'

Keke looked at him quickly. She was not playing the coquette; she just had never thought of it. That was the way she felt about men. She just accepted them as companions. She said, 'I didn't know. I'm sorry. I don't mean I'm not pleased or flattered,' she added hastily. 'But I – never thought of it. I like you very much and you've been very kind to me.'

Adebayo looked crestfallen, but said with a laugh, 'I'll get over it, I suppose; I'm still young.' He did not mean to sound offhand and Keke knew he was far from it.

'I think it's because you've been seeing so much of me. We'd better stop coming here,' Keke said.

So they stopped.

She was home on vacation. Her home was in a quiet village where things seldom happened. But this time something did happen. She met him at the village post office one day – a tall, overpoweringly handsome man. A mocking smile played at the corner of his mouth.

'Hello! We've been expecting you. You're the Hope and Glory of this place, aren't you? They lost no time in announcing it to me – everyone of them. I believe they'll make you their chief when you graduate.'

Keke should have been angry but she was not. There was something fascinating about him. She said, stupidly, 'You are a stranger here, aren't you?'

'Obvious, from my brilliant conversation. I'm on a visit to my uncle.'

'Oh you're even more conceited than I am.'

'Am I? Then we are two of a pair. I've been waiting for you to show me round the village. I mean "round" literally. There is nothing to see in the village itself except your father's mansion. You'll show me over the hills and valleys, won't you?'

So she and Chimele became friends.

They were dimly visible in the cold darkness of the night. His voice was pleading and she was replying in a cold, hesitant voice. He stretched out his hand to draw her nearer to him.

'No, no, no.' She shrank back.

He said, 'Will it always be no?'

'Tomorrow night,' she pleaded, and they moved away from under the tree.

In the twilight haze of dawn she lay in bed and gazed idly about her room. This was THE DAY. Her eyes fell on the wash-hand basin. It looked so cold, like last night. She thought of another night, the night that was yet to come.

'Father, if it be Thy will, let this cup …'

What blasphemy! She brought herself back with a bang. Horror! To compare that with Christ's Supreme Sacrifice! She left the bed and went to the wash-hand basin. She turned on

The Surrender

the tap. Slowly the water trickled out and wriggled into the outlet. Savagely she turned the tap faster. She hated wriggly things – like worms – and snakes. Snakes were cold too. She shuddered. The cold night, the cold sink, cold hospital floors, cold snakes, cold nights, Supreme Sac ... Sacrilege!

Again they were standing under the tree. His voice was tremulous with excitement. But there was no response in her. She tried to rouse herself but failed. He stretched his hands towards her. She began to shrink away.

'But you said tonight,' he said.

There was no answer.

'Don't you love me?'

'I do.'

'Then why don't you ever relax with me?' He was pleading again. 'You're so tense, like ... like ...'

Again they moved away from under the tree.

She lay in bed thinking. Why not? It was no Supreme Sacrifice but it would be a sacrifice all the same – a sacrifice of all the principles she has cherished for years. What are principles anyway? 'The world looketh on the outside, not the heart.' And if they said you did it, then, why not? Suddenly a terrible wave of hatred engulfed her – hatred for the idealist she had been. In childish pique she made her decision.

'I will do it,' she said. 'Then I'll deserve everything they've said.'

She expected all the agony of the past few days to melt away before her decision, but she felt uneasy. She fell into a mood of self-pity, moving into one of self-eulogy, then into one of self-condemnation. She seemed helpless under the interplay of emotions. Throughout the day she felt vaguely excited. Perhaps curiosity played a part in it.

They were again under the tree.

'There's a foodseller's shed quite near here and it's warm,' he said. He led her there with his hands round her waist. The shed was a mud affair with a leaky thatched roof through which they could see bits of the starlit sky. But it was good enough for their purpose, even though the ashes of the food seller's fire had blown all over the floor. They found a mat and spread it on the ground.

'Oh, Keke, why don't you say something? Are you angry with me?'

'Oh no, it's just that I feel strange, not having done it before.'

'Well, if it's only that ... anyway it's only for tonight you'll feel strange.'

They sat down. He started stroking her hair and worked downwards. When he touched her breasts, he could feel a slight tremor run through her.

'I'm beginning to wake her up,' he thought, flattering himself. He lifted up her skirt. She made no movement. He started kissing her passionately. It was not until he had been doing so for some time that he suddenly realized that there was no response in her. It would have been different if she had struggled. There was a certain brute joy in mastering a woman's resistance. But she neither responded nor refused. One does not become a realist in a day. Suddenly he stopped his wild passion of kissing, like a drunk made sober by an eye-opening occurrence. Cooly, he said, 'If there's anything I detest, it's cold-blooded murder, and next to that, cold-blooded sex. I may be a brute, but there are different grades of brutes.'

And he left her.

Keke was relieved that after all nothing had happened, but her victory was a pyrrhic one. On the way home she shed tears of humiliation. The following week she went back to college. The humiliating incident haunted her, but she felt safer in college. Her world and Chimele's would never meet again. He worked in the ministry of local government and she was the academic type. He had left her village, according to her mother's letter.

For a long time after term began, she avoided Adebayo, but in the end they drifted together again. He was president of the Lawn Tennis Club and she was the secretary.

One day Adebayo said, 'I still love you, you know.'

A cloud passed over her face.

Adebayo said, 'And I think you love me now. But there is something?'

She had a moment's panic. Should she tell him? No, she decided. Why bring the dead back from the grave? To her Chimele was dead; only his ghost haunted her.

Life went on pleasantly for Keke and gradually she forgot her humiliation. The walks to the reservoir were resumed. Once, as they were sitting on the ventilator, Keke said, 'Somehow I've come to think of this place as our own.'

Adebayo said, 'I feel like that, too.'

'I should hate to see anyone invading it.'

Then one day Keke walked up to the reservoir alone. Adebayo was to join her later. As usual, she walked with her eyes to the ground, so she did not see Chimele until she was a few steps away from him. He stood desecrating her precious retreat, a mocking smile playing on his lips.

'I see you still love the hills and the valleys. Who is it this time?'

She turned to go back and he seized hold of her. She struggled furiously.

'Leave me! Leave me!'

'Ah, there's some spirit in you, after all. That's more spirit than you showed that night.'

Keke stopped struggling.

Chimele said, 'That's better. You might as well be pleasant, as I shall be in college for two years. I've come down for the new local government course.'

All the hate which Keke had ever felt – hatred of the hostel girls, hatred of the cruel male students, hatred of society in general – was now concentrated into one blinding hate for Chimele. To her he symbolized all the forces of oppression, of humiliation, of scandal, that had always dogged her steps. And he would be there for two years, a constant reminder of a moment's childish pique. She would be blackmailed – until the end of life, perhaps. With all her strength she struck at him. He fell against the ventilator and lay still. Keke stared down at him. With a wild scream of terror, she turned to flee and bumped into Adebayo who had come up to the reservoir.

'What happened?' he asked, looking bewildered.

She did not reply but pushed past him blindly and rushed down the reservoir almost falling in her haste. She could see the hangman's noose, hear the news-vendors screaming 'Female Undergraduate Kills Boyfriend. Judgment today.'

She rushed into the hostel, fumbled in her drawer, found a bottle of tablets and swallowed twenty of them this time, to make sure. Then she lay on her bed.

Back at the reservoir, Chimele had sat up and was rubbing the back of his head. He looked Adebayo up and down insolently.

'So you're the new boy friend. What a change for the worse. You look like a boxer. Did you teach her to box?'

But already Adebayo was rushing towards the Women's Hostel. One of the girls came in answer to his knock.

'Is Keke in?'

'I don't know. I'll go and see.'

When she came back she said, 'Her door is locked.'

'I'm sure she's in,' Adebayo said.

The girl looked at him coldly and said, 'I knocked and knocked but there was no answer. She must be out.'

Adebayo stood undecided for some time, then left the hostel. 'I'll come back later,' he said to himself.

Back in his room he took up one of his textbooks and tried to study but he could not concentrate. He felt worried. Something about the way Keke had looked as she rushed past him made him feel uneasy. He remembered the *Scorpion* incident and rushed out of his room. In the women's hostel another girl came in answer to his knock on the common room door.

'I'd like to see Miss Ojeru.'

'I don't think she's in,' the girl said.

'But I know she's in,' Adebayo fairly shouted.

'How can you know that when ...' the girl began, but Adebayo was not listening. Ignoring college regulations, he

The Surrender

rushed to Keke's door and began to hammer on it. The other girls came out and watched open-mouthed as he started kicking the door. They thought he was mad. When he finally broke down the door and rushed in, he found Keke lying on her bed as if asleep. She wore a beautiful white dress. Adebayo rushed to the bed.

'Keke! Keke! Open your eyes! Look at me!' he commanded. He pulled her into a sitting position and shook her, but her eyes remained closed. He went on shaking her for some time but there was no response. Adebayo put her back on the bed and rushed out for help. The Hall Warden came and Keke was taken to hospital. This time she did not wake up.

The next day, one of the girls said, simulating sorrow, 'Isn't it very sad about Keke? You can do it once too often, you know. I knew a girl once, she kept on committing abortion.'

Bola

There were fourteen of us in the hostel – a motley collection of schoolgirls, schoolboys, workers and teachers. The proprietress, a kind, comfortable woman of about forty-five, was a clergyman's wife. Mrs Johnson had no children of her own. She had therefore thought of filling the big, empty vicarage with young people. Her hostel charges were fairly low so she always had a long waiting list from which she replaced the schoolgirls who went abroad on leaving school or workers who got transferred to other towns.

At the time of which I write there were eight girls among the fourteen hostel dwellers. Mrs Johnson gave us three rooms in a separate wing of the house and there we had great fun as is common among young people.

The life and soul of the group was Bola, a girl of seventeen who was taking a sewing course at one of the sewing institutes in Lagos. She was a beautiful girl, small, with a generous bust and a wonderful head of hair. Her eyes always twinkled merrily. Every evening she returned from her sewing lesson and told us stories she had heard from the other girls at the Institute.

One afternoon it was so hot we could not have our normal siesta, so we sat on the front balcony of the hostel from where we obtained a good view of the road. But hardly anyone passed along it. We were feeling bored and thinking of going back to toss on our mats when the gate creaked open and a young man walked into the compound. He must have been hugging the wall for we had not noticed his approach from the road.

His entry was a signal for an outburst of laughter. His pair of shorts seemed to have taken only a last minute decision to be shorts and not trousers. They were made of coarse grey wool and were held up to this chest by a red tie. His bright yellow shirt was too big for his body; the sleeves came down over his wrists. What seemed the crowning glory of this outfit was a faded red cap that was a size – just a size – too small.

Our laughter did not subside for a long time. The man walked up to the house oblivious of our amusement, and a moment later we heard a knock on the door. One of us, Titi, a schoolgirl, went to answer it.

She came back and said, 'He says he wants to see Bola.' We looked round for Bola but she was not there.

'But she was here a moment ago,' Titi said, and her look of puzzlement was mirrored on the faces of the rest of us.

'You'd better go and find her, Titi,' Aduke, a teacher and the eldest among us, said. 'She's probably gone to take some aspirin. She was complaining of a headache.' Titi went to look for Bola.

'It's funny,' Bimpe said, 'she's had that headache for a week. Ever since she got that letter, she's been looking miserable.'

'Perhaps her mother's ill,' I suggested.

'Her mother couldn't be ill because I know she died long ago,' Aduke said.

At this juncture, Titi came back and said breathlessly, 'I found her in the laundry room. She says she doesn't want to see the man. It's very mysterious.'

'Go and ask the man what he wants. Perhaps he's her brother.'

Titi went down again and from the speed with which she came back she must have taken the stairs two at a time.

'He says, he says he's her husband!'

There were shouts of surprise.

'I can't believe it!' Bimpe said.

'Good gracious! Married and us not knowing!' exclaimed Joko, a tiny fair girl, the youngest among us.

'Don't be silly, both of you,' Aduke said. 'He doesn't mean he's her husband. He means he's her fiance. It's the same word in Yoruba for both – with some qualification which is not always expressed.'

We were relieved but a little disappointed.

'Well, what are we going to do now?' Bimpe asked. 'Mrs Johnson is away.'

Aduke said determinedly, 'Leave it to me,' and went downstairs. She was away for a long time and when she came back, she looked worried.

'I couldn't do a thing. She absolutely refused to see him. So I went and talked to him. I tried to be tactful and said Bola was ill. But apparently he'd seen her streaking across the compound. He said he would go and talk to her. I showed him where to find her and left so as not to embarrass them.'

She had hardly finished speaking when we saw the man come out from the side of the house and walk back towards the gate. We could not see the expression on his face as his back was turned to us but even that back was expressive of his disappointment and unhappiness.

'I asked him to let me know when he was ready to leave,' Aduke said with a break in her voice which was the nearest I had seen her come to weeping. As for Joko, she simply burst into tears.

'To think that we were laughing at him,' she sobbed. An air of great tragedy enveloped all of us. When the proprietress came back, Aduke told her about the incident. It then came out that the man was indeed Bola's fiance – 'intended', she called it – and he had been paying for Bola's keep and her sewing lessons. Ojo was a pupil teacher somewhere in the provinces. He had been engaged to Bola ever since she was a child. He had sent her to school and then to Lagos to learn sewing.

The proprietress was most sympathetic. She called Bola and spoke to her. But Bola's stand was unrelenting. She would not have anything to do with the man.

'Will she have to leave now?' Aduke asked. Mrs Johnson replied, 'He's paid for her sewing lessons up to the end of this year. There's still three months to go. After that ...' She shrugged her shoulders.

For days we talked about nothing else but Bola's problem. Reactions were varied. Some of us, led by Aduke, felt that it was a sad situation because definitely Bola was now much better off socially than Ojo. Her being ashamed of him was understandable whilst on the other hand Ojo himself could hardly be blamed for wanting to marry a girl to whom he had been engaged for years and on whom he had spent so much money. Bimpe and two others felt indignant about it all. It was presumptuous of Ojo to think still of marrying Bola. She was much more civilized than he now. When they remembered how he had dressed, they shuddered. 'I couldn't live with such a man,' Bimpe declared, 'I'd simply murder him one day.'

As for Bola herself, for days she went about the house hardly speaking to anyone. Whether she was just sad or felt ashamed because we had seen Ojo, we could not say. She continued to go to her sewing lessons.

One month passed and then two, and it was less than a month to the end of the year. The question, unspoken, was in the air. After December, what? Bola had no money of her own.

On January 1st, we all watched Bola to see whether she would start packing. She didn't. In fact, she was in very high spirits. We thought Mrs Johnson was waiting for the New Year celebrations to end before sending her away.

But January came to an end and Bola was still with us. We then worried Aduke into asking Mrs Johnson what had happened. She came back and reported, 'Her boarding and sewing fees have been paid for three months. She paid herself.'

We were astounded.

Then the truth came out. Bola had acquired another boy friend who had promised to marry her and pay back Ojo's expenses. Every evening Bola started returning home later than usual. The new boy friend returned her every evening in different cars. Bola became secretive and was frequently seen day-dreaming on a pile of planks in the compound.

'Bola has surely got herself a millionaire,' Joko would say, wistfully looking at the new car which had just stopped at the gate.

I don't know who started the story but somehow it was in the air that Bola was to be married soon. Mr. Akinyemi continued to come for her in different cars and we were all full of envy.

One day Bimpe went to see off a cousin who was going to England by boat. We were all in the room when she came back.

'I saw Mr. Akinyemi today,' she said to Bola and we wondered why she should speak about him. By tacit agreement we had all refrained from talking to Bola about her new acquisition.

'Whom was he seeing off?' Bola asked. Her eyes shone at the mention of Mr. Akinyemi's name.

'He wasn't seeing anybody off. He was going away himself. He has left for England. Didn't he tell you?'

Bola fainted and was taken ill. The doctor came and said she had been pregnant for four months. Then we discovered the truth about Mr. Akinyemi. He had been coming for Bola in borrowed cars!

Mrs Johnson reluctantly asked Bola to leave. She was kind enough to give her a small sum of money and her fare. Aduke was in the room when Mrs Johnson spoke to Bola. She came back and told us what had happened.

'Mrs Johnson thought she would have hysterics, that was why she asked me to be present. But, do you know, she took it very calmly! I was so surprised and so was Mrs Johnson.'

That evening the proprietress was summoned urgently to the hospital. She took me with her. We found Bola in one of the side wards, looking very weak and tired. We found out she had tried to drown herself and that had brought on a miscarriage. She was lifeless and spoke to us in monosyllables. I did not know whether she rejoiced or not at the loss of a baby she had not wanted. Mrs Johnson gave her the things she had brought – bananas, biscuits and orange squash – and we left.

And everyday Ojo came to the hostel and asked after Bola. Mrs Johnson would not let him go to the hospital for fear of exciting the poor girl and causing her more pain. But when he heard that she was well and was coming home he insisted on being allowed to see her.

'Not for the first two days,' Mrs Johnson stipulated.

The day he was allowed to see her Ojo came in a suit. It was not the best he could have worn but it was respectable enough. He wore it rather diffidently, it is true, but certainly, he did not present the ridiculous figure that had first sent us into peals of laughter the first day he appeared. I took him to Bola where she was lying on the sofa. Her eyes were shut but she said, 'Come in.'

We went in and Ojo rushed to her side.

'My poor girl, my poor, dear girl,' he said brokenly. 'Look at me, please. I'll do anything for you. I'll learn to be the kind of man you want. Look at my suit – do you like it?'

I could have laughed at his words but somehow I didn't want to. I saw Bola open her eyes and look at him. She smiled – a painful, sad smile – as she touched his hand.

The Feast

She looked at herself in the mirror. An all-embracing look from head to toe, from side to side, turning first to this side, then to the other. She even tried to look at her back by twisting round. This was not satisfactory so she went into the bedroom and brought out the other mirror. With both mirrors she could see all of herself well.

She was a pretty, young woman, plump and cuddly, with a round face set on a neck which had a tier of small folds that was considered a mark of beauty among her people. Whenever she smiled, the small gap in her upper incisors gave her a coquettish look. She was looking festive now, with her special new wrapper which she wore over layers of beads tied below her navel, thus emphasizing her already full bottom, while red paint judiciously applied to her arms and legs gave her a glow that suggested warmth and passion.

Putting the hand mirror down on a stool, she hitched up her wrapper more firmly and readjusted her headtie so that two ends stretched out on either side of her head like the wings of a bird. Then she took up the small mirror again and gave herself a long last look in both mirrors. Satisfied now with every aspect of her attire she put both mirrors away and sat down by the door to wait. Her husband had already gone with the men to make preparations for the final ceremony of the festival and she was now waiting for her friends to pick her up in the canoe.

As she sat Mayo thought about her husband. She was daily growing to hate him more and more. He did not ill-treat her but what he had done was worse, unforgivable. She thought back over that night so long ago – the night of her shame. She could hear the sound of the drums again, beating, beating, gloating over her shame and nakedness. She could see the torches as they lit up the faces of the dancers. Everybody was happy except herself. She could see the bridal bed now, a primitive affair built of mud but with a rich spread of layers and layers of woven cloth. The top one had a bridal scene woven into it – a circle of drummers in the middle of which a man and a woman were dancing opposite each other.

But as she sat waiting for her bridegroom she did not feel the elation and excitement which she ought to have felt as a young bride. Instead, her heart was pounding so hard she thought she would choke. After some time the drums stopped and there was sudden silence. The door opened and the bridegroom entered. Before he shut it Mayo caught a glimpse of several women standing just outside. They would remain at their post till the marriage was consummated, she knew. Panic assailed her. Should she throw herself at his mercy and tell him? He might understand and forgive her. But when she looked into his face she did not dare. Perhaps he would not know, she concluded hopefully.

Meanwhile he stood by the door, looking at her. He was a tall, handsome lad and the voluminous white loin cloth embroidered with blue motifs sat well on him. On his young face was a look of expectancy, an excited yet restrained look as if he was not sure of himself. He stepped further into the room and slowly unwound his loin cloth. He hung it on a nail behind the door and stood in his underwear. Shyly he came towards her, hands trembling slightly with anticipation. He blew out the hurricane lantern and she could hear him undressing. Then he came to her. Outside, the drums began again, their rhythm now a dull, monotonous beat. If only they would all go away, Mayo thought, if only this were tomorrow and nobody else here but she and Kande, she might be able to explain. But with all these people waiting ... she shivered.

'Are you cold?' Kande asked, solicitous.

'Yes, I am,' Mayo agreed, quickly catching at this straw, thinking he would leave her alone if he found she was ill. But he took it in a different way.

'I'll make you warm,' he said and began fondling her breasts.

Mayo shivered again. 'I'm not well,' she said. 'Couldn't we wait till tomorrow?'

'And all those people waiting outside, what shall we tell them?'

Outside, the women nodded to themselves and said she must be virtuous; it was taking so long. The drums warmed up to a stirring rhythm.

Inside, a struggle was going on in the bridal chamber. But the young man was not daunted. He had been told what to expect. 'They always fight at first,' an old uncle who had six wives had told him, 'but don't you take any notice. Just carry on.'

And carry on he now did. He pushed her flat on the bed and she fought back with all her might, as she had been told all virgins did. But in the end she was subdued. And Kande got the shock of his life. He was a young man who thought highly of his family standing and this seemed to him an unpardonable affront on the part of his parents-in-law, sending him damaged goods.

For one moment Mayo thought he would strangle her as he gripped her neck with both hands. But he did not. Instead he got up quietly and dressed, while Mayo lay on the bed too frightened to move. He lit the lantern, then opened the door. The women standing outside nearly fell into the room. 'The sign!' they shouted, 'Where is the sign?'

'Ask her,' he said, and walked away.

The women poured into the room, 'Shame on you, shame on you,' they shouted at Mayo who was now cowering in a corner of the room.

After the uproar had died down Kande sent Mayo back home. He refused the propitiation money and demanded the return of the bride price he had paid.

And Mayo lived her days in shame. When she went to market the women would giggle and wrinkle their noses at her. At home she fared no better for her parents hated her now for having brought shame on them. So when Kiru came along to ask if he could marry her, they jumped at the offer.

He was an elderly-looking fisherman and lived up the river. Of unprepossessing looks, he was also deadly dull. He looked rather weather-beaten and spoke very slowly as if it took a long time to fashion each word in his brain. Mayo's parents asked for no bride price but simply gave their daughter away as a gift – which was the greatest humiliation a girl could suffer. But Mayo was past complaining. She went with Kiru, hating him with all her heart for coming to save her from ignominious spinsterhood. She did not see that an evening's indiscretion should be paid for so dearly as she was now doing.

Being so pretty, she wanted beautiful things – beautiful wrappers, beautiful ornaments, delicious food, a proper house, and a husband whose looks did not make her shudder each time he came near her. She shuddered now as she thought of him, his long fingers groping for her in the darkness of their bedroom, like the tentacles of an obscene animal. But he had given her respectability, her parents told her, and for this she must be grateful.

Presently, voices floated across the water and a canoe emerged from behind the trees. It drew up on the bank and a chattering, noisy group of women jumped out and moved towards Kiru's hut. Their noise and their frivolously-tied headties gave them the appearance of a crowd but they were actually six. As they came towards the hut, Mayo left her post by the door, scrutinized her face once more and came out. Together they went into the canoe. With the women singing heartily, the canoe pulled out into midstream.

The festival generally lasted seven days and this was the seventh day, the culmination of all the previous six days' feasting and merriment. There was to be a big sacrifice of fish to the god of the river and afterwards a big dance on the river bank.

All the men were already assembled in a little clearing among the bushes by the river. A single drum was beating monotonously and here and there a head nodded to the beat. When the women arrived they gave a shout of greeting which the men returned in a more subdued manner. The women then stood opposite the men.

The Feast

There was a hush. Even the monotonous drumming had stopped. All eyes turned towards a hut in the clearing. The drum started again, this time louder, rising in pitch and building up to a frenzied crescendo. A youth wearing a short loin cloth tied round his neck, carried the big fish into the clearing on a large wooden tray. He was followed by a priest dressed in a white loin cloth with his upper body and legs painted with white chalk. Behind him came another man bearing a knife in its sheath on a small wooden tray. The procession now approached the shrine in the centre of the clearing – a stone slab raised on a mud-and-stone pillar. When the procession reached the shrine there was sudden silence. The youth laid the big fish on the slab. The priest took out the knife from its sheath and sliced open its belly in a single movement. He spread the fish flat. A loud shout came from both the men and the women. The priest then split bitter kolanuts on the fish and poured some oil on it, all the while muttering incantations.

And all the while Mayo gazed at the shrine. A casual observer watching her intent gaze might have thought, 'What a religious woman, absolutely fascinated by the sacrifice.' What fascinated her, however, was not the sacrifice but the youth standing by it. He was the most beautiful thing she had ever seen. He had an athletic figure and a face whose handsomeness she had never dreamt was possible. He stood perfectly erect, a half-smile on his face – a copper-coloured god. Once he looked away from the sacrifice and encountered Mayo's rapt gaze. He turned away immediately, but occasionally he looked at her and his face wore a quizzical, half-amused look. Mayo's heart beat faster.

The priest finished his incantation and the youth put the fish back on the tray and, bearing it shoulder high in front of him, led the procession to the river. The priest chanted a monotonous song all by himself and the youth threw the sacrifice into the river. It sank out of sight and the men and women raised a shout that must have been heard in the next village. Chanting a light, melodious song they went back to the clearing and dancing began. At first the priest danced a slow, dignified dance, then the youth and one or two other men joined him and danced a fast formation dance while the women swayed rhythmically to the beat and the rest of the men tapped their feet impatiently. In the end everybody joined in the dancing.

Mayo slipped away from the assembly.

When the dancing was over and the noise had dwindled away across the water, Mayo came back. The youth was clearing away the sacrificial things. He straightened up from his task and looked at her for a moment, then said, 'You were at the ceremony, weren't you?'

She nodded.

'It was very good,' he said.

'Very good,' she repeated.

'And the fish was the biggest ever.'

'The biggest ever.'

She seemed to be talking mechanically.

'My name is Moneka,' he told her. 'I'm training to be priest. My uncle wants me to.'

'And you?' she seemed to awaken from her dream.

'I have to obey my uncle.'

There was a pause, then Mayo said, 'I'm stranded.'

'So I see. Where did you go? Didn't you enjoy the ceremony?'

'There are better things in life than ceremonies.'

'Such as ...?' He moved nearer.

She cast her eyes on the ground.

'Such as you,' he completed for himself. 'I noticed you among the women.'

And that was the beginning. From that day on Mayo and Moneka had clandestine meetings. When her husband was away fishing at night Moneka came in his boat and went away before her husband came back. Mayo's temper improved and she became indulgent towards her husband. She endured his lovemaking by pretending to herself that it was Moneka. The petulance was gone from her face and the peevishness from her voice. Kiru thought, what a difference approaching motherhood made in a woman.

Which made it all the more terrible when he discovered the cause of all this sweetness.

He had gone fishing one night and discovered that he had brought out the wrong net. He went back for it and, thinking he should not disturb his wife, crept in by the back door. It was then he heard voices, his wife's lilting voice and a man's baritone punctuated by laughter. He thought of the unborn baby that was not his and his first reaction was to grab the knife with which he gutted the fish he caught but he realized he would be no match for the athletic youth. He stole out of the house again.

The whole of the next day Kiru spent on the river in his canoe. When he came home in the evening he had someone with him. From the kitchen Mayo heard their voices as they approached the hut and wondered whom her husband could possibly be bringing along with him. She went round the side of the hut to see and came face to face with Moneka as she turned the corner. Shocked, she said, 'What are you doing here? Why have you come with him?'

'It's all right and above board,' Moneka said airily. 'I'm here as a benefactor, not – well, you know.' And his eyes twinkled merrily.

'But – but how? I mean, what happened? How did you meet him?' Mayo fired the questions at him rapidly.

'Well, you see …' Moneka began, but Kiru came round the side of the house opposite the route Mayo had taken.

'This young man saved my life, wife,' he said, putting down the empty basket he was carrying. 'But for him you would be a sad widow by now. You'd better thank him.'

Mayo curtsied before Moneka, according to the custom. 'But, what happened?' she asked. Kiru explained, 'I was in midstream when my boat sprang a leak suddenly – I think something sharp jutting out of the river must have punctured it. The boat was fast filling up and, try as I could to bail out the water, I knew it would soon sink. I could have jumped out and swum but, well, I'm not as young as I used to be. I don't know for how long I could have held out if Moneka hadn't been in a nearby boat. Well, he rescued me and brought me home,' Kiru concluded. 'You will stay to supper won't you?' he added, turning to Moneka.

Mayo tried to hide her disappointment. Moneka was a fool, why didn't he leave Kiru to drown? That would have solved their problem. Resentfully she went to prepare supper. They had a meal of boiled plantain and pepper sauce and afterwards the two men sat talking outside in front of a log fire, for it was harmattan time and the evenings were cold. Mayo busied herself about the house trying to subdue the thrill she felt on seeing Moneka.

And so Moneka became a friend of the family. Quite frequently he came over in his uncle's canoe and, until Kiru could build another canoe, they fished together in Moneka's canoe.

At first Mayo did not know whether to be pleased at this new situation or not, but as time went on she began to feel frustrated and tantalized by the constant presence of Moneka around her while she could hardly get him alone or even talk to him since it was not the custom for women to join in men's conversation.

But one night when Kiru had gone fishing alone in his new boat, Mayo heard the front door open – it always creaked as it opened. She went to see if Kiru had forgotten something, but instead of Kiru she saw Moneka and rushed into his arms.

'At last, at last,' she cried, clinging to him.

'It's been so long, hasn't it?' he said, 'so near and yet so far apart,' he joked.

'I'm sure you didn't miss me as much as I did you,' Mayo said pouting.

'Because I joked?' Moneka asked. 'Just wait and I'll show you whether or not I've missed you.'

And after their passions had been exhausted, they talked.

'How much longer's your training going to take?' she asked him.

'Another six months.'

'And then you'll become a priest?' Moneka did not answer.

There was silence for a long time, then Mayo said reflectively, 'You won't be able to fish any more and that means I can't see you any more'.

Still Moneka said nothing.

'Does your uncle not want to know what you use the boat for so often, and at night too?' Mayo wanted to know.

'My uncle? Oh he doesn't suspect anything. I told him I have to help a sick friend with his fishing.'

'And he thinks you are a good boy as a result, doesn't he?' Moneka laughed.

'But if he should discover, won't he be terribly angry and curse you?' Mayo asked. 'A priest's curse, you know, and with justification too.'

'Don't worry about that. Things will be all right before it comes to that.'

Long after Moneka had left, Mayo pondered over this enigmatic statement, trying to drag some meaning from it.

Kiru came back from his all-night fishing trip the next day a completely different man. He had two friends with him and he seemed much more lively than his normal self. He sent for palm-wine and sat down all morning drinking. He called his wife to him and made her sit on his knee.

'You're shaming me, husband,' she said, trying to pull herself away, but he gripped her tightly and she could not move. The friends laughed coarsely at this. When Mayo was able to free herself she was terribly shaken. Could he be mad? she thought. It wasn't unusual for old men to go mad when they lived such lonely lives as Kiru lived, or used to live. She thought she must find Moneka quickly and ask his advice. If Kiru was going mad she must leave him. But where could she go? Certainly not home. That was impossible. She went to where Kiru was lolling on the mat with his friends and asked if she could borrow his boat.

'I want to go and see my mother,' she said.

'Your mother – he, he,' Kiru said with a drunken laugh. 'Your mother – ah, yes, you must visit her. Yes, you must visit home. How long will you be away?'

'Six hours.'

'Stay six days.'

'No; six hours will be enough.'

'Do you hear that?' he said turning to his friends. 'She says six hours will be enough. Ha, ha, ha.'

Mayo got into the boat quickly and pushed off, paddling not across the river as she would normally do if she was going to her mother's place, but in the direction of the priest's hut. She rowed powerfully, impelled by her fears. The quietness of the atmosphere seemed to mock the agitation in her mind. The sun had not yet become hot and the air was fresh. She rowed very close to the bank, seeming to find the bushes protective. She needed protection very badly now. An anxious thought came to her — suppose Moneka was not at home?

But he was. The priest's hut was on a slight rise and from there it was possible to see any canoe drawn up on the beach.

Moneka must have been standing in front of the hut looking towards the river, for before Mayo could drag the canoe up the bank he had bounded down and was dragging it up for her.

'Thanks be to the gods you're at home,' Mayo said, almost fainting with exhaustion.

'Is there anything wrong?' Moneka said. 'You shouldn't be doing this in your condition. Tell me, has he found out?' He looked into her eyes.

'I – I don't know,' Mayo said in a shaky voice, 'all I know is he is mad – and drunk too. He laughed when I told him I wanted the canoe to go and see my mother and he said I could stay six days.'

'Perhaps he suspects,' Moneka said.

'What can I do now?' Mayo lamented.

Moneka thought for a moment. 'Come into the hut,' he said. 'The master is not in. He's out at a private ceremony up the river. He won't be back for another four hours.'

They went into the hut, bending low as they passed through the doorway so as not to bump their heads against the door lintel. Moneka sat Mayo down on a low mud seat and said, 'You must be thirsty. I'll fetch you some water.'

He disappeared into an inner room and Mayo looked round her. The room was rather stuffy with only a small window. The overcrowded floor was cluttered with calabash bowls and dusty bottles. Over in a corner stood a carving about three feet tall. It was of an indeterminate colour owing to the various libations that had been poured over it, but its shape was unmistakable. It was that of a fish standing upright with its tail erect and to the side. But somehow it wore a human expression that made it look sinister. Beside it was a bottle of palm-oil, a rafia basket with a lid and a long butcher's knife in its sheath. There was a continuous dripping sound and Mayo tried to find out where it came from. As her eyes roamed round the room it fell on a long-necked gourd nailed to the top of the door. It was no bigger than a man's fist and wrist but it was the most frightening object in the room. It was coated with a white furry substance from which some liquid was dripping and yet the furry substance remained as it was, undiminished. Mayo shuddered.

'Aren't you feeling well? Moneka asked, coming back into the room with a calabash bowl in his hand.

'It's – it's that thing,' Mayo said, pointing at the object.

'I don't like it either, gives me the creeps. Here, drink this.'

She drank deeply and returned the bowl. 'But how can you become a priest if you feel like that?' she asked.

He took a stool and sat opposite her. 'I'm not going to be a priest,' he said, deliberately.

'But – but' Mayo could hardly believe her ears.

'If I become a priest, it would be difficult for me to see you. I want us to go away together.'

'Oh!' Mayo said and covered her face so that he might not see the joy on it.

'What's that?' Moneka cried suddenly, jumping up. 'I heard a noise – footsteps, I think.'

'The priest must have come back,' Mayo cried in terror.

'Wait,' Moneka said and went out.

He was gone for about five minutes. When he came back he looked puzzled. 'There's nobody outside,' he said. 'I went round the house and looked in the bushes, but I couldn't see anyone. But there's a new boat drawn up on the beach. Trouble is, there are too many bushes around here.'

Mayo got up. 'I think I should go back now,' she said.

'Think you can paddle back all that way?' Moneka asked.

Mayo assured him she would be all right. 'I've rested enough.'

'I'll come and see you soon,' Moneka said. 'To make arrangements. It will take time, though. My uncle has to find someone else.'

When Mayo returned home Kiru was out, but he soon came back. 'I went with Ahine to his mother-in-law's place,' he explained. 'She's making trouble between him and his wife. How was your mother? And your brothers?'

Mayo told him they were all well. Surprisingly he did not seem drunk now, though his eyes were bloodshot.

After this Kiru became extraordinarily loving to his wife. He embraced her in public, chaffed her pleasantly, and paid her every attention – all of which she detested. He pestered her with so much attention that she hardly had time to see Moneka. He came home unexpectedly and made her anxious and worried, wondering whether he knew. Occasionally he kept out of her way and then she had a long, uninterrupted period with her lover. And after that came the husband's attentions again. This alternation of pleasure and pain kept Mayo on tenterhooks and destroyed her peace of mind. Her pleasures were always spoiled by fear of her husband's coming attentions.

Then Kiru announced that he was going to have a feast. 'In honour of the child,' he said.

'But it isn't born yet,' Mayo protested.

'What of it, it's going to be born, isn't it?'

'He's mad,' Mayo thought, terror gripping her heart. 'He's really mad.'

But he seemed to be happy. He whistled about the hut, redecorated the roof with new thatch and made plans for the

The Feast

feast. 'I don't want you to do the cooking,' he told his wife. 'My sisters will do it and send the food across.'

Mayo tried to protest again about the feast but he silenced her. Of late she had not dared to oppose her husband. A guilty conscience had cowed her completely.

The day of the feast came and all the people of the village turned up. They thought it strange that a man should be holding a feast for an unborn child but at the same time they could not miss the chance of a good feast at another man's expense. There was no known taboo against it. And so they came. It was a bright, sunny morning with not a cloud in sight and the sound of the river was a pleasant hum to the ear.

The food was lavish. There were dishes of lentils, there was corn cake and there was *foofoo* accompanied by a fish stew with an aroma that filled the whole place as it was borne in an enormous bowl by one of Kiru's sisters.

The male guests sat down together in the open air and the women sat a little apart from the men, according to the custom. Everybody seemed happy and the men cracked coarse jokes among themselves in loud voices while the women looked modest and pretended not to hear. Kiru was in high spirits, supervising the drinks and giving directions to his sisters.

Mayo sat among the women and wondered why Moneka had not been invited. Could something have happened to him? 'Oh come soon and take me away,' she prayed. She wondered where he would take her. He had told her his priest uncle was a maternal uncle. His father's home was on the other side of the river up on the hills. His people were farmers, growing yam and maize in the heavily-watered valley between the low hills. His father was dead but there were still some distant cousins living there, she believed. She wondered how she would adapt to a life of farming; she who had been so used to the water and to going everywhere by boat. There was one nice thing, though, she would not have to eat fish. She had come to associate fish with Kiru coming home at dawn and, despite his exertions on the water, insisting on coming to her still smelling of fish. Even his very breath smells of fish, she thought.

Her husband's voice broke into her thoughts. 'Look at Mayo,' he said, 'Isn't she radiant?' He was sitting among the men and he was acting jovial as became the host at a feast. He drank from the calabash of palm-wine in his right hand, wiped his mouth with the back of his left hand and belched loudly. The male guests smirked at Kiru's remark and made coarse jokes about Mayo's obvious condition. Kiru seemed to find the jokes amusing and Mayo looked confused. Then one of the guests said to Kiru, 'This is a good feast.'

He looked round at the other guests who all nodded in agreement. The speaker went on, 'That nice young man who goes fishing with you sometimes – didn't you invite him? I don't see him here.'

Kiru said, 'You mean Moneka – he's here all right.'

The guests looked round. 'Here? We can't see him.'

'He's not right here, but he's nearby,' Kiru replied with an enigmatic smile.

'Come,' he added, getting up.

Puzzled, the guests followed him. When they got to where the women were sitting, he said to Mayo 'You come too.'

She followed him, looking bewildered. One or two of the women followed too out of curiosity. Kiru led them all through a path in the bush behind the house until he reached the grove where the family shrine was. He stopped.

'There he is!' he said, a mad look in his eyes. The eyes of the crowd followed his pointing finger. And they saw Moneka's head staring at them from the stone slab which served as the altar. In front of it, laid neatly like a pair of gloves, were Moneka's fingers.

In stupefied silence the guests looked at the head, then after what seemed an age they looked at one another and their eyes were full of questions. At last, as if at a signal, they all turned towards Kiru. He was standing with his feet wide apart, his arms at his sides, hands clenched. A gloating look was on his face. 'Yes,' he said, 'I killed him. Won't you ask me why I killed him?'

An elderly guest said, 'Why did you kill him? He was like a son to you.'

Kiru replied, 'Does a son steal his father's wife?' There was a gasp at this and all eyes turned towards Mayo, no doubt expecting to see guilt and shame written on her face. Instead Mayo rushed at Kiru shouting, 'You've killed him, you monster.' She dug her nails into his cheeks and bit him in his left arm. He gave a wild animal yell of pain and lifted her up to dash her to the ground. To save herself she grabbed at the knot of the loin-cloth tied round his neck. She clung to this so desperately that when he tried to fling her down they both fell. The crowd surged forward but as hands made to grab them, Kiru jumped up, ran a few yards away and bent down. When he straightened up he was holding an axe. There was blood on it, presumably Moneka's. The advancing crowd saw the axe and halted. Kiru stood over his wife as she lay in the dust, her wrapper undone, revealing her left breast, full, the aureola very dark. Mayo shut her eyes expecting every moment to feel the axe on her neck. When she did not, she opened her eyes. Kiru said to her, 'I'm not going to kill you. That would be too good for you. I want you to carry the shame of this day with you until you die.' He looked at her big belly, big and rounded inside the wrapper, and spat at her. 'You were an outcast from your family. Now you will be an outcast from the community.' With this he walked away into the bush. The crowd melted away.

Mayo lay in the dust and as she felt the first pains in the small of her back she cried out in anguish even though the pain was not yet severe, 'Oh, I wish I were dead! Why doesn't someone kill me?' But there was no one with her. They had all gone away and she was all alone with her burden.

Man of the House

Tonight Odafen was able to read in peace. She was lying in bed, her short, tubby husband Demola snoring beside her. He never read books but glanced through the day's newspapers, reading only the headlines and that did not usually take long. 'This is my sacred hour,' she thought 'and tonight is particularly sacred.' It was an unusually peaceful night. The chattering of birds on the nearby trees had ceased and no nightbird disturbed the quiet. The bats which nested under the eaves of the house had apparently decided to join the day creatures for their usual squeaks were not heard. Even the frogs in the nearby marshland were not croaking. She did not mind the chorus of the female frogs but she found the loud croak of the bullfrog jarring. Tonight there were no petrol explosions that shook buildings and shattered windows. There were no rat-tat-tat-tat sounds from anti air-craft guns practising just in case …

Suddenly the peace was no longer perfect. Quick light footsteps dented the peace and Odafen wondered why anyone would be running at that time of night. Just one pair of footsteps. The steps went past the front of the house and stopped by the bedroom window. The dent became a hole that widened and grew into a large tear. 'Help me!' a girl's voice cried. At the same time she beat her fists on the window.

Odafen put down the novel she was reading. It seemed she could hear sounds up the street. 'My God, they're coming,' the girl's voice screamed as she beat frantically on the window. 'They are coming! The soldiers are coming. Please open the door. Help me in the name of God!'

Odafen's heart was beating fast as she started to get up. Her husband had woken up and, seeing her getting out of bed asked, 'What are you doing? Where are you going?'

The girl was now sobbing hysterically. 'E jo o! E jo o,' she was pleading.

Odafen went to the door. Her husband's voice rapped out, 'Don't open the door.'

'But we can't leave her out there. They may kill her. Remember yesterday?'

Yesterday ...

She had woken up with a start. The pounding that had woken her up was coming from the house opposite. It was midnight – the hour when witches are said to fly about. She saw some figures. They were not witches but they were witch-hunting for she heard one of them order, 'All midwestern Ibo traitors in this house, come out!'

There was a pause, then the landlady looked out of an upstairs window and asked, 'What do you want?'

One of the four soldiers standing in front of the house pointed his gun up. 'Are you deaf? We said all midwestern Ibo traitors in this house should come out.'

The landlady said, 'There are two midwestern Ibos living here but they are no traitors. They have been living here for a long time.'

'All midwestern Ibos are traitors,' another of the soldiers said. He had a coarse voice which made one think of sandpaper scraping on wood.

'Are you going to open the door or not?' The first soldier asked in a voice that showed he was losing his patience. 'We don't want to come in but if we have to force our way in ...'

A third soldier said, 'We don't want to harm you. Just send out the traitors.'

'And we shall deal with them,' the fourth soldier said. 'We must teach them not to be traitors.'

The landlady closed her window and there was a pause. After some minutes the gate into the yard opened and two men came out dressed in trousers and shirts. One was still tucking in his shirt while the other was buttoning his fly. The soldiers pounced on them, hitting them with the butt of their guns and pushing them down.

'Lie down! Lie down!' their leader ordered.

The men prostrated themselves.

'Not there! Here!' the leader snapped, indicating a spot near the open gutter. The two men lay down, their noses inches from the green scum that covered the stinking, stagnant water. Both the third soldier and the fourth soldier had whips in their hands and they started flogging the midwesterners. At each stroke the men's heads jerked up but the other two soldiers used the butt of their guns to push them down again. The beating went on for some time, an involuntary gasp coming from the victims' throats at each stroke. After five minutes the first soldier ordered the men, 'Get up!' They got up slowly and painfully and the soldiers marched them off.

All this Odafen and Demola saw from behind the curtains of their ground floor flat. They watched in silence as the men were marched away. The whole street was silent except for the crunching of the soldier's boots on the gravel which covered the road. Surely people could not have slept through all that pounding on the door; they must all be hiding behind their curtains, Odafen thought. Like us.

She turned to her husband, 'Will they kill them?' she asked.

'How would I know?' he replied irritably, 'I'm not in the army. I'm going back to bed.'

And he did. His head had hardly touched the pillow when he was snoring. But Odafen could not sleep for the rest of that night. The civil war in the eastern part of the country which Ojukwu had renamed Biafra had seemed so distant until the Midwest Region was invaded by Biafran soldiers. There was a strong suspicion that some Midwest Ibos had aided their kinsmen in the east across the River Niger and this had led to the witch-hunting.

Odafen grew more and more resentful as she listened to her husband's quiet snoring. How could he be so callous? He was stupid too, swallowing every silly story he heard in town about the conflict. She remembered the evening he had come back early from work just before the war started to announce with great trepidation, 'Ojukwu is going to bomb Lagos tonight.'

He had rushed home early, contrary to his habit, not out of concern for her safety but because he felt safer at home. Why was he so gullible? Couldn't he ever reason in spite of his years at the university? Why had she ever married him? There was really no need to ask herself that question. She knew. He had threatened to kill himself if she did not marry him. She should have realised then that he wanted a crutch, someone to lean on in his inadequacy. He came from a broken home and needed a mother figure.

She told him coldly, 'Who told you that? Ojukwu will not bomb Lagos with thousands of Ibos living here.'

She had been proved correct. Soon after this incident Ojukwu had summoned all Ibos back home and when almost all of them had left, he had proceeded to attack the city using guerrilla tactics – explosions near a cinema house, a bomb dropped on a petroleum plant, and so on. When she referred to her earlier statement, he had remarked bitterly, 'She's bloody right as usual.'

That was all in the past. Today ...

Odafen opened the door and the weeping girl precipitated herself into the house. Odafen locked the door, turned and looked at the girl. She could not be more than fifteen. Odafen knew she lived in a house at the other end of the street. She looked so vulnerable, standing before her, shivering in her short, cotton print nightgown, her round brown face contorted in fear.

'What's the matter?' Odafen asked her.

'I was sleeping, we were all sleeping,' she began in a trembling voice, 'they started banging on our front door. They shouted, "Open! We are soldiers." I was afraid. I thought they had come to kill us. I jumped out of the window and ran to the back of the next house. It was dark. Then I saw your light. My God! They are coming here!' Fresh terror made her run behind Odafen as many footsteps approached the house, crunching on the gravel. She clung to Odafen's waist.

'You see,' Demola said reproachfully. 'You see what your bedtime reading has caused, *acada* woman. She passed many houses before she got here. It's because she saw the light. The other houses were all dark.'

They heard confused noise outside. Then the words, 'Where is she? Where is the girl?' The next moment there was pounding on the door. 'Open the door!' a voice said peremptorily.

Odafen said to the girl, 'Go to the bedroom. There.' The girl rushed into the bedroom and shut the door. Odafen went to the door and opened it. Two soldiers were standing before her and several more had surrounded the house.

'Where is the girl?' one of the soldiers asked. 'She must be here. We've checked all the other houses and she's not there.'

Although her heart was beating fast, Odafen tried to act calm.

'Why were you chasing her?' she asked.

'Because she is Ibo. Bring her out immediately.'

'I know this girl; she's a Yoruba girl.'

'If she's not Ibo why did she jump out of the window? We didn't know where she went at first. Bring her out.'

Odafen put on her pleading voice.

'Well, you see, she is a young girl and she was frightened by the pounding at the door. It's past midnight, you know.'

They seemed to accept her explanation. 'We want to see the girl, anyway,' the leader said.

Odafen went and brought the girl. 'You see how young she is,' she said.

The soldiers started to leave and the girl knelt down and thanked Odafen for saving her. But the two soldiers came back and the one who had not spoken asked, 'Where is the man of the house?'

It was then that it occurred to Odafen that she had not seen Demola since she went to open the door. She had been so preoccupied with saving the girl. She thought quickly. It was probably safer for her to give the impression that her husband was out but then nobody went out any more at that hour of night. That was why so many nightclubs had shut down. In any case a husband was no protection these days when husbands had been made to watch their wives being raped. And how would she explain the fact that her husband had avoided the soldiers? Would they not become enraged on seeing him? She said to the soldiers. 'My husband is dead. I am a widow.'

The two soldiers looked at her, not with pity but with respect.

'Well, Madam,' said the leader, 'you don't need a man in the house. You are more than a man yourself.' They again turned to go.

Suddenly there was a loud crash inside the house. The soldiers rushed into the living room and Odafen and the girl followed them. Part of the ceiling had collapsed and Demola was lying on the floor in the midst of fallen debris. He must have landed on his left hip for he was holding it with both hands, his face full of agony.

'Madam, but you said there was no man in the house. You said you were a widow. Who is this?'

'My husband,' she admitted, feeling ashamed. 'I could not tell you the truth.'

'And what is the truth?' the leader asked in a severe tone. 'Why did he hide in the ceiling? He must be Ibo.' He cocked his gun at Demola on the floor. 'Tell me quickly, is he Ibo? Is he Ibo?'

Odafen looked at her husband with contempt, then turned to the soldiers, 'No, he is not Ibo. He is only a coward.'

A Child is a Child

Similade was feeling elated as she sat in the 'owner's corner' of the official Peugeot 505 car which she now rode as chairperson of the National Children's Commission. The Children's Day rally at the Tafawa Balewa Square had gone very well. It had been a cool morning – cool enough to make the long parade of selected children from fifty schools in the Lagos metropolis less tedious than it would have been in the hot tropical sun. Spectators had not had to fan themselves with their programmes, a spectacle she had always detested. A colourful parade followed by callisthenics which spelt out various slogans about children's welfare. The children had marched past in uniforms of various colours and designs, their leaders displaying banners on which were inscribed the names of their schools. The police band had risen to the occasion by playing with verve and charm, both new tunes and old favourites such as 'Ni-ke, Ni-ke' and 'Old Calabar'. When these two favourites were played, the children had changed their stiff marching to rhythmical swaying that silently echoed the music. And who could blame them? Many of the spectators, made up of teachers, parents, social welfare officials, educational authorities and members of the general public, had been similarly moved, dancing in their seats, the floating ends of women's headties waving like little flags as their heads moved this way and that to the compelling rhythm. She herself had been tempted to join in the swaying but had felt that in her position as guest speaker, she should look dignified – like the Special Guest-of-Honour beside whom she was sitting. He was the Deputy Head of State, a civilian in a light grey flowing agbada robe with the front lavishly embroidered with dark grey thread. She herself was more simply dressed – in a navy blue brocade *boubou* with light blue embroidery round the neck. Her headgear was equally simple – a turban made out of the same material. She was glad she had chosen this outfit in preference to the body-hugging 'up-and-down' outfit made up of a long skirt and a fitted overblouse which she had originally brought out of her wardrobe. The *boubou* not only made her look more motherly as befitted the occasion, it also protected her from the cold, sweeping wind of the open arena as she went up to the dais to give her address.

She had worked hard at her speech which was not designed for the rows of children now standing before her for they hardly listened to grown-up speeches, anyway, but was directed at her adult audience, including the ones who would be watching it live on television or listening on their radio sets. Her message was for them. It was the outpouring of her soul. She wished she could discuss in detail all the problems that plagued young people in the country, but there was no time. However, she was able to mention quite a few – hunger, neglect, child abuse, female circumcision, sex discrimination in education, child marriage, and the insecurity of broken homes. She waxed emotional as she talked about the paradox of the Nigerian child whose arrival was celebrated with great jubilation only for them to be treated later with neglect and lack of understanding of their needs.

'In this country, a home is not complete without a child. In all our cultures, the birth of a child is an occasion for jollification – for eating and drinking, for singing and dancing. The child is given many names, some of which indicate the circumstances of its birth while others are prayerful hopes for its future. But what happens after all the eating and drinking, after all the drumming and dancing, after the showers of good wishes with the symbolical tasting of the good things of life by the new babe – salt and honey for a sweet life, red palm oil for good nutrition and as a balm for softening the harsh realities of life, *orogbo*, kolanuts for a long life and so on? What happens after all this? For a large number of children in present day Nigeria, these are wishes that may never be fulfilled. Why else would infant mortality be so high? Why would there be so many children roaming the streets during the day and sleeping under bridges at night? What about the thousands of child hawkers, particularly girls, exposed to the dangers of child abuse by adults who lure them into corners with money or by pretending to look for change? Is this a question of poverty or of misplaced priorities? Our attitudes towards children must change. Children should no longer be regarded as status symbols, as unpaid domestic help, as an insurance for old age, as funeral undertakers to ensure a befitting burial with its financially crippling protracted ceremonies.

'We need to change our orientation and realise that if we bring children into the world, we owe them a responsiblility to cater for their physical well-being, for their spiritual growth and their emotional needs. There must be more children's hospitals and clinics, more child welfare centres, more facilities for children to develop their talents – whether in the educational and creative areas or in the arena of sports. Every child must be given equal opportunity to grow up with a sense of belonging, for only then can children become balanced adults who can contribute meaningfully to the development of their country. We must all contribute to this sense of belonging – as parents, teachers, educational policy makers, and social welfare workers. There must be no discrimination between one child and another. As my grandmother always said, "A child is a child." And I think my grandmother – bless her soul – was one of the wisest people I ever knew. I do not need to spell out the different ways in which some children are marginalized in homes, at school and in the society at large. We all know them. But I would like to stress this. Whatever happens between a man and his wife, the children must never be made to suffer. The interests of children must be paramount.

'Finally, I would like to thank the Federal Government for appointing me chairperson of the National Commission for Children. The Commission has mapped out plans for carrying out the different actions that must be taken to improve the lot of the Nigerian child. We are however hampered by poor finances. We need help – in cash or in kind – and look forward to receiving such help, not only from the government, but also from concerned individuals and organizations. I thank you all for your patience.'

Many people had come to congratulate her at the end of the ceremony but though she was pleased at the reception of her speech, it was the announcement by the Deputy Head of State that had made her day. He had said that a children's welfare fund would be set up by the government. Similade saw in this announcement the consumation of her advocacy of better treatment for the Nigerian child. Her commission did not lack ideas but lack of funds had been the constraint.

Enveloped in euphoria, she was about to leave the square when a tall, slim middle-aged woman with a face that must have been beautiful once but which now seemed to be distorted by a permanent sneer, came up to her with purposeful steps and said belligerently, 'Simi, what was all that nonsense you were saying, "A child is a child"? Well done, missionary woman. I hope the government gives you a national award. That fund business is another *chop-chop*, isn't it? Are you proposing to build a gigantic children's welfare centre with millions of naira? Remember me O, when you are giving out contracts. Me too I want to chop O. I will give you your kickback. How much per cent – ten or is it now twenty?' And she walked away, tossing her headtie in the air.

Similade was not angry. Rather, she felt sorry for her old friend, Jokotade. She could understand her feelings. Similade had not seen her since that awful day at the burial of Jokotade's late husband, a judge of the high court, a personable man who gave powerful sermons at church as a diocesan lay-reader. At the funeral service which took place in the Cathedral, the first ten rows of pews to the right of the central aisle had been filled by legal luminaries and lesser members of the legal profession who all wore white wigs and black gowns. Eight rows on the other side of the aisle had been occupied by members of his church society, The Morning Star Society, all dressed in white agbada and black caps – a contrast to the legal crowd.

The archbishop had preached the funeral sermon in which he painted a glowing picture of a public-spirited man of great intellect whose humility and exemplary life made him a veritable model for others to copy. Similade had felt proud on behalf of her friend who wore a black silk dress with a lacy veil over her face. What happened at the cemetery had therefore been a shock. Family members were supporting the weeping Jokotade when they noticed two other women dressed in widow's weeds weeping profusely on the other side of the grave. The women turned out to be other wives of the deceased who had married one according to Yoruba customary law and had performed muslim rites with the other. He had married Jokotade in church. The end of the burial ceremony had ended in chaos with each widow trying to tear the others' eyes out. Jokotade had been particularly embittered by the fact that one of the widows had been an old classmate. She had instituted a lawsuit challenging the right of the six children of the other women to share the judge's legacy with her own two children. The case was still in court and it was rumoured that from the day of the funeral Jokotade never visited any of her women friends. She considered every one of them a potential traitor.

Similade therefore forgave her embittered former friend her cutting words and insinuations. But she had always wondered how her friend could have been so trusting, so naïve, that she had not had any suspicions about her husband's infidelities. She must be stupid, Similade thought.

The driver opened the back door of the car and she stepped in, cheerfully determined that nothing, nothing at all, would be allowed to mar the wonderful day. The driver said, 'Madam, which road we go take – Third Mainland Bridge or Eko Bridge?'

Similade consulted her watch, then realized it was futile. There was a time when it took eight minutes at most to get from Tafawa Balewa Square to Yaba via Third Mainland Bridge. Eko Bridge, which was the second to link the island with the mainland, had always been congested since it led to the densely populated Surulere, Mushin and Agege areas. Third Mainland Bridge had always been her choice when the odd and even number system was operating and motorists whose registration numbers began with an odd or an even number used the bridges on alternate week days and took taxis on the forbidden days. Then came the downturn in the economy and many old cars went off the roads and those people who still had functioning cars heaved a sigh of relief at the free flow of traffic. Later, some bright person got the idea of importing used cars called 'tokunbo' cars because they came from overseas, and the roads became so terribly congested, with bottlenecks at spots where some of the imported decrepit cars had broken down, that driving on either bridge became a nightmare. There was Carter Bridge, of course, the oldest bridge, but the self-styled Area Boys had taken over its approach, extorting money from motorists at intervals along the route. A dangerous set of older street-children, Similade thought to herself.

'Take Eko Bridge,' she told the driver. If you had to spend two hours doing the ten-odd kilometres from Lagos island to the mainland, you might as well do so on a bridge that offered some entertainment. Eko Bridge was really a combination of an overland flyover and a bridge over parts of the Lagos Lagoon. It skirted the long Marina waterfront, crawling parallel to the big shops and the banks, hovered above Isale Eko where the indigenous Lagosians live, swung right, then dipped at the busy Ereko wholesale and retail market for manufactured foods, climbed up again and dashed towards Iganmu, famous for its beer brewery and the National Arts Theatre shaped like a brigadier's cap, then cruised along Western Avenue towards Ikorodu Road which led to other parts of the country. It certainly was a more interesting route than Third Mainland Bridge from which the main view was a dirty lagoon cluttered with weeds and ugly floating logs, with waterside shanties ruining the foreground of modern skyscrapers.

Similade had a fairly smooth ride on Eko Bridge until her car approached the Marina shopping centre after which the traffic moved by fits and starts. At each traffic hold-up, popularly referred to as 'go-slow' by Lagos motorists, street hawkers crowded round their windows, pressurizing them to buy their wares. Some of the hawkers were in their teens.

They often had to sprint for their money whenever the cars suddenly started to move. At least they get a lot of exercise, Similade thought.

The hawkers sold all kinds of assorted goods. Eko bridge had become an elongated outdoor department store. Electric wall clocks, car accessories, kitchen ware, pressing irons, children's wear and toys, battery lamps, television antennae, assorted biscuits, sportswear, underwear, reconstituted dried milk in cartons, and fresh shrimps dripping with melting ice were a few of the goods that were thrust at them. Similade was thankful that the air conditioner in the car worked and so she could keep the windows wound up. In Ibadan whenever she drove her own personal car, which had no air conditioner, heavy bunches of plantain and bananas almost landed on her lap or came dangerously close to her glasses while she remonstrated with the fiercely competing teenage hawkers. She was also thankful that the official car had such a good driver with quick reflexes so that he was able to avoid colliding with the reckless drivers of *molue* buses with their battered bodies and inefficient brakes. These deadly *molue* buses driven by daredevil drivers had a habit of either roasting their passengers alive or plunging them into the lagoon. The plunging incidents had become so rampant in recent times, especially on the new extension to the Third Mainland Bridge, that the government had proposed making sacrifices to Olokun the water goddess and building a shrine at the foot of the bridge. This had aroused a controversy between Christians and members of the traditional religious sects. 'Why don't they check the speed and the brakes of the *molue*, for goodness sake?' Similade thought irritably. Of late the role of bus conductors of these vehicles had been taken over by street boys who gave the drivers wrong 'go-stop' signals and created more chaos on the roads. At the bus stop before the National Stadium on Western Avenue, one of the new-breed conductors, a boy of about eleven, was standing beside his bus, beckoning to would-be passengers and shouting 'Fadeyi, Obanikoro, Maryland, *e wole.*' Since many other *molue* bus conductors were shouting in a similar manner, the noise was deafening. The buses had caused a hold-up because many of the drivers refused to queue up in the bus bay but preferred to take in passengers right on the road. Similade's car and other cars had to wait. Suddenly a motor-cyclist who was threading his way between the stationary vehicles, brushed against the outflung arm of the bus boy who had been shouting 'Fadeyi etc.' Shouting imprecations, the boy ran after the motor-cyclist and slapped him, then rushed back to the bus. The motor-cyclist looked infuriated but could not leave his motor-cycle and chase the boy, nor could he ride against the one-way traffic. He therefore contented himself with making a rude 'waka' sign at the boy with his hands flexed like the claws of an animal about to attack a prey. The boy reciprocated the sign, reinforcing it with the words 'Your father and mother bastard too.'

'That boy should be in school studying, and learning good manners,' Similade thought, 'not being corrupted by the riff-raffs that hang around bus stops and motor parks.' Her commission still had a lot of work to do – clearing children off the streets and stopping under-age employment.

The bus conductor banged his hand on the back of the bus and the bus began to move. It was filled to capacity and three passengers were standing at the open door gripping the doorframe. As the bus gathered speed, the conductor swung onto the bus between the passengers at the door, hanging on precariously with one leg and one arm, the other leg and arm dangling in the air. One or two bus conductors had fallen off before and died but this did not deter other boy conductors from showing off. Some of them, of course, smoked Indian hemp, which was a great pity, Similade thought. Another problem for her commission.

The Commission appointment had been a surprise to her as she had not been consulted. These days people heard about their appointment to public office on the radio, and later got an appointment letter, which usually ended with 'congratulations', leaving no room for rejection. Not that she would have rejected it even if she had been consulted beforehand. Indeed, she was very pleased about it because she had led the campaign for its creation and it had taken the Federal Government such a long time to take a decision. She had almost begun to despair of its ever being set up. Therein had lain the surprise.

She and her husband were in the upstairs living room when they heard the news. Instinctively she had looked at her husband to see how he would react. There had been a moment's silence before he grinned and said, 'Congrats, Madam Chairperson. Your dreams have come true.' He had got up and given her a pat on the shoulder. Then he said, 'I'm going downstairs to lock up.'

'Was he displeased?' she wondered. Kayode and she had been married for fifteen years and had four children – two boys and two girls in that order. All were doing well in their studies. Theirs had been a fairly uneventful marriage. They'd had their little quarrels, of course, as was to be expected in any marriage but nothing serious. Quite early in their marriage they had agreed never to go to bed angry. This had been made easy by the routine of family prayers at dawn and at bedtime, a habit they had acquired from their homes, his father being an archdeacon of the Anglican Communion and hers a knight of the Roman Catholic Church. They had both attended mission boarding schools.

Similade could hear her husband shutting doors and sliding bolts. Then he came up. He was approaching fifty but he looked much younger with his athletic figure and boyish face. She still loved him after all these years. She herself had not worn so well because she was addicted to pastry which made her overweight. However, one of her assets was her face with its high cheek bones which could take almost any hair style. Her Bob Marley plaited hairstyle with its two hundred strands was sometimes woven round her head like a halo, sometimes bunched on top of her head, at other times draped loosely over her shoulders. Kayode often complimented her on the various arrangements, not realizing that she made the changes to save her the trouble of spending six hours having the hair re-plaited after washing it. She was too busy.

That night after they made love, she had said to him, 'My new assignment – I have to do a lot of travelling. You won't mind, will you?' His reply had been, 'You know I have the consultancy and I've been travelling too. In fact, I am happy because now I shan't feel guilty about my frequent absences from home.'

Her husband had again travelled out of Ibadan, that was why he had not gone to the rally with her. Was he back yet? She now began to feel tired and sleepy, and was dozing off when the driver's voice woke her up. 'Madam, let us buy petrol here. This is the last petrol station before the toll gate.'

They pulled into the filling station, and joined a short queue. Three attendants were working the pumps. A week earlier, when the perennial petrol shortage was still on, they would not have dared delay until they got to the last filling station. In the few places where petrol was available, often there was only one pump serving motorists and motorists double parked along the roads causing more 'go-slow'. Similade had never been able to get over the fact that a country which produced billions of barrels of petroleum could not satisfy its citizen's needs. Some of the *molue* buses which caught fire and roasted their passengers alive had been carrying plastic cans full of petrol.

They got petrol in a couple of minutes and the driver drove onto the highway. Once past the toll gate, Similade closed her eyes and did not open them until they got to the Ibadan toll gate. It took some time for them to get to New Bodija where they lived. As their car approached the house the driver sounded the horn. Her daughters came out and the elder, Foluke, unlocked the gate. She said, 'Kabo, Mummy. You were wonderful on T.V.' Ore, the younger one said, 'Bunmi and Tola watched with us and they both said you were great.' Bunmi and Tola were their neighbours' children.

The driver stopped the car in front of the house and Similade came out. 'Where are your brothers?' she asked.

Foluke said, 'They said they would watch from their friends' houses but they are not back.'

The house-help had prepared lunch and they sat down to a meal of rice, beans and chicken stew, topped with an ice cream dessert. She took a generous helping of ice cream, wishing she did not have such a sweet tooth. After lunch she went upstairs to lie down and read a book.

It was the sound of her husband's car on the gravel outside that woke her up. Her book had fallen to the floor. 'Oh, I must have dropped off,' she said to herself and rushed downstairs to meet him. The boys had returned and one of them opened the door. Their father came in carrying two suitcases which the boys took from him. As Similade hugged her husband she noticed a boy of about six and a girl of about eight hovering behind him. The boy was carrying a small suitcase while the girl had a sling bag over her right shoulder and a carrier bag in her left hand. In her usual breezy manner she said, 'Hello, children,' then turned to her husband and asked in a low voice, 'whose children are these?'

Her husband replied, 'They're mine. They've come to live with their brothers and sisters. Equal treatment, you know. After all, a child is a child.' Similade stared at her husband for a moment, then collapsed into a chair and burst into tears.

The Vitamins

Ranti Olumide was having a drink on the verandah of his Ikoyi reservation quarters when he saw the boy approaching. He was dressed in clean but oversized clothes from which his thin arms protruded like sticks. He swayed as he walked, his big head perched on a thin neck like a mushroom. Ranti thought, 'This boy reminds me of something – something ...' Yes, he reminded him of the Judas effigy which he and the other neighbourhood boys carried and whipped all over the Obalende area, chanting about the treachery of Judas – 'Judasi, Ole, O pa Jesu je, ole.' Good Friday was a day for collecting pennies. The Judas effigy had swayed in the same way as this boy was now swaying. The boy looked harmless enough but he told himself that he must remember always to padlock the gate after his late afternoon walk. He took the walk because of his sedentary job as a bank manager and was thus able to retain his figure.

'Good evening, Sir,' the boy said as he came to the foot of the short steps leading to the verandah. 'My papa sent me to you, Sir. He said you should give me job as your houseboy.'

'Who is your papa?' Ranti asked.

'Tailor, Sir. Tailor at Abule-Ijesha, near Mamma's place.' As he said this he climbed up the steps and leaned against a pillar.

Ranti remembered now. 'Tailor' as the whole neighbourhood called him, was an Ibo man who lived with his family of six, three doors from Ranti's mother's house. His wife Ada was one of those beautiful light-complexioned women from the eastern part of the country who, because they married early, still retained the bloom of youth after four, five, six children. 'Tailor' was not a handsome man and Ranti's wife Bisi always referred to the couple as Beauty and the Beast. However, their children had sensibly taken after their mother. But right now, their eldest son was not a beautiful sight to look at. His face was puffy and covered with blotches. He looked very unhealthy and did not seem to have much energy.

'Oh, Sammy, I'm happy to see you. How is your mother? And your brothers and sisters? So you all survived the war.'

'Everybody is well, Sir.'

Ranti turned and called in a loud voice, 'Bisi, come out and see who's here.'

Bisi came to the front door wiping her hands on a napkin. She had been cooking in the kitchen. She was a slim, pretty woman of thirty-seven. Her husband was eight years older.

Ranti said, 'Guess who this is.'

Bisi retorted. 'You tell me, I have something on the fire.' She was not too pleased to see the miserable creature.

'That's Sammy, Tailor's first son at Abule-Ijesha. His father sent him to live with us.'

Ranti saw the shock on her face but she said with great warmth, 'Ah, Sammy, you've grown bigger. How old were you when you all returned to the east?'

'Thirteen, Madam,'

'So you're now sixteen. Quite a big boy.' She was desperately trying to make him feel better.

'So how's your beautiful mother? And your sisters and brothers?'

'Everybody is well, madam,'

Bisi had her doubts. You're not a specimen of good health, she thought.

Sammy became a member of the Olumide household. Ranti took him to the hospital and was relieved when the doctor diagnosed kwashiokor and prescribed vitamins. He had thought it was something infectious which his two children, Busola and Yomi, could catch.

In no time, with nutritious food and vitamin supplements, Sammy lost his bloated and blotchy look and began to regain his good looks. When he was fully recovered, Bisi thought, 'Now he can help with the housework.' But Sammy had become used to idleness. He was usually to be found reading the newspapers or chatting loudly in the boys' quarters with his new-found friends. Bisi was irritated. She said to her husband, 'When this boy looked half dead he had no friends. Now he is fine and doesn't need their help they have all turned up calling themselves his brothers.'

'Poor man no get brother,' Ranti quoted philosophically, then added, 'I'll talk to him.'

One day, a letter arrived from Sammy's father. It said:

Dear Sir and Madam,

I hope this letter meets you in good health. I am sorry to say our condition here is not good. Sammy's mother is very sick. Doctor say she must have plenty vitamin but we not have money to buy vitamin. All our money lost in the war. We know you are taking good care of our Sammy and may God reward you plentifully, but as Yoruba people say, "If you sew dress for lazy person, you must dye it so it not look dirty" because he cannot wash it every time. We need your help again. Please send vitamin quick quick so Sammy's mother not die. I beg you in the name of God.

Yours in Christ, Charles Okeke.

Ranti and his wife discussed the quickest way to get the vitamins to the desperately ill woman. Christmas was approaching and many people were already travelling to their hometowns for the festival. Ranti went to see Papa Chukwuma who now lived in Tailor's old house. He knew of one Papa Bomboy who was leaving early the next day for Nimo, Tailor's hometown. He would send to Papa Bomboy to expect the parcel of vitamins but Ranti would have to leave home early to get to Iddo Motor Park and hand it to him. Ranti thanked Papa Chukwuma for his help and rushed off to get the vitamins.

The next day he drove Sammy to the park with the parcel of vitamins and went off to work. As he drove along with the cool breeze blowing onto his face through the open windows, he felt good both outside and within himself. That lovely woman would not die for want of a few vitamins.

But die she did. Two months later Papa Chukwuma brought Tailor's letter announcing the sad event and ending reproachfully with 'I thank you again for taking good care of my son. That is enough. I must not ask for too much.'

The Olumides were puzzled.

'Didn't she get the vitamins we sent?'

Papa Chukwuma was startled and said, 'Myself, I been tink before say you no' send the medicine. Papa Bomboy say he no' see Sammy for motor park. He wait, wait so tey. He wait long time the bus nearly leave him for park as he go look see whether Sammy dey come.'

Ranti called Sammy before them. He wore a stern face as he asked peremptorily. 'What did you do with the vitamins we gave you for your mother? She is dead.'

Sammy covered his face with his hands and started snuffling.

Ranti said severely, 'Stop your crocodile tears and answer my question. What did you do with the parcel of vitamins?'

Bisi added, 'And don't tell any lies because we have checked with Papa Bomboy. You never gave him the parcel.'

After a moment's silence, Sammy admitted sullenly, 'I sold them in the market.'

Bisi shouted, 'You sold the vitamins meant to save your mother's life? How could you do a thing like that? How could you do a thing like that?'

How could he do a thing like that? Sammy's mind went back to the three-year civil war, to the well-fed 'attack' women who were trading back and forth between Federal lines and Biafran lines and sleeping with enemy soldiers who stole relief materials meant for a kwashiokor-ridden population including – no, especially – children. He was one of those children and nobody had pitied him. An aunt of his was among the 'attack' traders and when he asked her – no, begged her – for some food, she had laughed in his face and said, 'Tell your mother to do as I do. It's every person for herself.' That was the lesson he had learnt from the war – every person for herself, or himself, as the case might be. You had no father, no mother, no brother, no sister. You were all alone. Of late he had been feeling the stirrings of manhood. His friends had taken him to a beer parlour in Mushin and they had spent the money from the sale of the vitamins there. And here was this woman screaming at him, 'How could you do a thing like that?'

The One Who Came Back

When I was a teenager cemeteries had a peculiar fascination for me. Where other girls quickened their steps and turned their eyes the other way on going past a cemetery, especially at night, I would stroll boldly in and sit on the graves and write poems, or what I thought were poems. Thus I came to know a great many people, both living and dead. And somehow it was the dead who fascinated me. They exuded an atmosphere of romanticism which I found intriguing.

I lived next door to the old Ikoyi Cemetery in Lagos, and when I wasn't playing table-tennis I was in the cemetery. I would sit at the foot of a grave and read the inscription on the headstone and wonder what sort of a person the occupier had been. Had he been a kind man or did he beat his wife? A name here might give the impression of a retiring, gentle disposition, whilst another would suggest wickedness, strange midnight rites and drunken orgies. Some of the graves had heavy chains round them and I was told by one of the gardeners that these were to keep the occupants from coming out and haunting people as they were known to be wicked in their lifetime.

I often watched the grave diggers at work. 'Who's dead?' I would ask. They would tell me. And when the funeral party came I was there. There were two types. There was the quiet little group which came to bury their dead and went away after doing so. There was also the big funeral party complete with choir and clergy in front and, behind, giggling girls and chatting women in white dresses and black or navy blue hats attending their third or fourth funeral that month. After the funeral they lingered around the cemetery, buying bananas and lemonade from the hawkers.

I saw many a graveside scene with a lot of weeping and wailing and unrestrained, inconsolable grief. Sometimes a mourner tried to throw herself into the grave and a mild commotion would ensue. But somehow these people did not move me. It was those who came afterwards that filled me with a peculiar, tender feeling. I mean the ones who came back the second or third day, or even the following Saturday or Sunday, singly, sometimes with a bunch of flowers and sometimes without. This was real grief, real desolation, I felt, and even now whenever the picture of those genuine mourners rises in my mind I am filled with a kind of sweet sadness.

I shall never forget one of these pilgrims. She came one Sunday morning while I was trying to write a poem. As soon as I saw her I put the pad away. She was simply dressed in a grey cotton frock and grey shoes which seemed to harmonise with the greyness of dawn. She was slightly built with a kind of calm beauty that filled you with tenderness. Her oval face was quite composed and she walked with sedate steps. I wondered whom she could have come to see among the dead. Was it some lover? I thought of a friend of mine whose fiance had died suddenly. For days and days she had shut herself up in her room weeping, seeing no one and eating nothing, and when in the end she was persuaded to come out, all the passion had been drained out of her and left her face calm like this pilgrim's face.

The girl moved about the graveyard reading an inscription here, an inscription there, and my eyes followed her. But somehow she did not strike me as an idle gazer. I got up and started strolling too. Soon a gardener came along and she went across to him. I moved near them so as to hear what she said.

'Do you know where Mr Valentine Adewunmi was buried?' I heard her ask and her voice was like her face, calm and soft with a hint of sadness. 'He died on the fourth.'

The gardener scratched his head and slowly shook it. Then he waved his hand vaguely in the direction of some family vaults. 'Perhaps he is there.'

The girl said, 'I don't think he was buried in a vault.'

I thought it was time to remedy the gardener's

incompetence. Coming from behind a grave I said, 'I know where the grave is. It's on the other side. Come, I'll show you.'

She was very grateful and we walked along the narrow path, she behind me.

I remembered the young man's funeral very well. It was his name that first struck me. I was at an age when I could still be fascinated by such a romantic name. I had gone as usual to the cemetery and begun looking round, picking out a new grave here, giving graves which had caved in a wide berth, and reading the card labels in the glass wreaths. I had asked one of the gardeners if there were any funerals on that day. They had taken to digging the graves in advance so a dug grave was no indication of an impending funeral. The gardener had informed me that one young man, Valentine Adewunmi, was going to be buried that day.

'The boy na fine boy. You see am so, 'e be like sun. Ah, but Death 'e too wicked. I be gardener for 'im papa house before. 'Im papa get plenty houses but the one whey den live for Yaba, if you see am 'e be like palace. Dem get plenty money. The boy die for accident, na 'im papa kill am.' He sighed heavily.

I was shocked and asked the gardener to tell me exactly what had happened. He told me.

'The ting 'appen like this. 'Im papa 'e get many many lorry. Some dey go for Ijebu, some dey go Ilesha, one 'e go for Enugu. Na the one wey dey go for Enugu kill am.

'The boy 'e stand for corner street near dem house, 'e dey talk plenty plenty with one girl, den dis lorry dey reverse. The driver 'e no' see the boy and the boy 'e no' get ear again for hear lorry because the girl 'e too fine. Na 'im dis lorry reverse 'e kill am. Im mamma nearly die. Den don carry am go for hospital. Ah, but Death 'e too wicked! Fine, fine boy like that.' He shook his head sadly.

And it had been a grand funeral, for the boy's father had been a member of the Island Club, the most prestigious club in the city at the time. The coffin had had silver handles and a well polished mahogany body. I thought to myself, 'I don't remember seeing this girl at the funeral.' Of course I couldn't have seen her. There were such a lot of girls. Evidently a very popular young man.

I stole side glances at the girl. She still looked calm but a sort of purposeful expression had also come into her face. I thought to myself, 'Poor girl, she must have been out of town when death took him tragically away and now she was coming to have her own private funeral. Or perhaps she was the only one who had really cared?'

'Did you know Valentine well?' I asked her. It seemed so natural to call him Valentine.

'Yes,' she answered.

'He was a very popular young man,' I said, trying to please her.

'Yes, *very* popular,' she agreed, stressing the word 'very.'

I looked at her quickly and found that her face now wore a half-smile.

'I'm so sorry he died in that way,' I continued.

'And sorry he died at all, aren't you?'

I was surprised at this reaction and was still trying to fathom the meaning when she went on, 'Did you know him well too?'

'No, not at all,' I said hastily.

'That's funny,' she said.

We now came to the grave and none too soon for I had been getting slightly disconcerted by her questions and remarks.

The grave had just been finished and had a beautiful white headstone with this inscription:

'In Loving Memory of
Valentine Olufemi Adewunmi
Eldest son of
John and Agbeke Adewunmi
Died 4th April, 1946,
We shall never forget.
By his Parents.'

The top of the grave was a tray of beautiful white marble chips. Resting on the stones were some glass wreaths.

'It's a very beautiful grave,' I said, offering consolation.

The One Who Came Back

Her face seemed to be working and she was twisting a handkerchief round her little finger. I thought she might want to be alone with her grief, so I withdrew.

I had not walked far when I heard a peculiar crunching sound and the sound of broken glass. And added to this was the smell of burning paper. I walked back and was shocked to find her dancing over a heap of burning paper on the grave. The glass wreaths had been wrecked. As I moved nearer I saw on her face a look which I have not seen on the face of any human being since. It was a combination of hate, fury, triumph and disappointment. I could have called one of the gardeners or the caretaker but I didn't. I had heard of love transcending all things – even the grave – and it had seemed to me an overwhelming thing, but hate that transcends even the grave was – oh the pity of it! She was having her revenge but the poison was still there. I prayed to God, 'Please take away the bitterness.'

By the Silent Stream

She was sitting on a log of wood staring into the water when I saw her, a young woman of about twenty. She was not dressed for travel for she did not wear a headtie. There was a child on her back and the child appeared to be sleeping. All round there was the peculiar stillness of the forest at noon. Not a breath of wind, not a sound of birds, just the quiet, unbroken reflection of branches and leaves in the muddy stream.

I moved nearer. She must have heard the sound but she did not turn round. Her chin on her hands, she continued staring into the water.

'Good afternoon,' I said, as I approached her.

'Welcome,' she answered and her voice was toneless.

I began to wonder what she was doing on the bank of the stream, in the middle of the forest, kilometres from anywhere. It was not a place I would have chosen myself to rest in for the leaves had rotted and a dank smell filled the air. If my car had not broken down, I would not have been walking in that place. But the next village was eight kilometers on the other side of the stream and I was going there hoping I could find a mechanic.

'Can you ...?' the woman's voice broke into my thoughts. It sounded doubtful.

'Can I do what?' I asked, smiling down on her, for she intrigued me. I thought of a hundred and one requests she could make – tell her the time, lend her my flask cup for she carried a bottle of water on her lap? But what she said was: 'Can you help me dig a grave?'

I was taken aback. 'Dig a grave?' I cried and my eyes fell on the baby on her back. She followed my gaze and said quietly, 'Yes, he's dead.'

I couldn't think of what to say. 'I'm sorry,' I said after looking at the baby for some time.

'Why not take it home?' I asked.

'I can't go back home,' she said, 'and I can't go forward. It's forbidden in our clan. You mustn't take a dead baby across water.'

I still hesitated. I wasn't sure I would not be breaking a law by helping her to bury the child.

'I'm sorry I can't help you,' I said and started to move away.

'In that case I shall have to stay here till I can find someone who can.'

I thought of her sitting there all by herself, the dreadful burden on her back, not even able to cry – her grief too deep for tears. And I went back.

I went back to my car and took out a matchete which I always carry with me on tour in case a tree falls across the road. I dug a shallow grave under a big tree and together we laid the child in it.

'I've got to go now,' I said to her.

'Goodbye, and may the Lord of Heaven reward you.'

On getting back to the stream with the mechanic much later I was surprised to find the woman still on the log. I went across and said to her: 'Why, what are you still doing here? Why haven't you gone?'

She spread her palms on her lap, face upwards. 'What is the use? They won't want me anyway. At least, not now that the child is dead.'

'Look here,' I said, 'suppose you tell me the whole story? Perhaps, I shall be able to help.'

'No one can help me,' she said.

'Come, come, don't talk like that. No one is ever beyond help. Not if the Almighty wishes it. Tell me how the baby died.'

Reluctantly she began ... 'My husband killed the baby.'

I was shocked.

'You see, he's a drunkard, and when he's drunk, he doesn't know what he's doing. Look.'

She bared her left arm and I saw the marks. Long streaks of scars on the flesh.

'Look here too. He did that with a blade, and rubbed pepper in it.'

I had already noticed the scar on one cheek and wondered which ethnic group carved marks on one cheek only.

'And look at these too.' She bared her right thigh.

But I had seen enough. Her otherwise beautiful medium-dark skin was a mass of scars, long dark streaks, darker than her normal colour.

'And the baby?' I asked.

'I was coming to that. That happened this morning. My husband woke up at dawn and started drinking *ogogoro*. By the time I was awake he was already drunk. When he heard me stirring he came over and shouted down at me on the mat. "Just waking up, are you? Lazy slut." He kicked me with his foot. I didn't say anything, knowing the mood he was in. I got up quietly and took up my baby. My husband went on railing at me. I was giving the baby its bath when he yelled at me. "Come here, Abunovbo."

"I'm coming," I shouted back. "I'm giving the baby its bath."

"Come here, I say, you daughter of a bitch."

"I'm coming," I yelled back. 'You know the way it is when you're giving a baby its bath in the morning. You can't leave it exposed. Besides there was soap all over its body.'

'I heard my husband get up from his chair. He rushed at me and I snatched up the baby from the tub.'

"Huh. Think you'll protect yourself with the baby, eh? You're wrong."

'He yanked the baby from me and flung it on the floor. Then he came at me. I snatched up the baby and the bottle of water near it and ran out of the house. The baby was not dead yet but I knew it was surely going to die. I didn't stop running till I'd gone a long distance. I wanted to go to his parents and show them what their son had done.'

Her voice had become excited as she told this part of the story.

'I tried to walk very fast,' she continued. 'The baby's breathing grew fainter and fainter. I walked faster. But I couldn't walk fast enough.' Her voice dropped. 'The baby died just before I got to the stream.'

'You should have taken the dead baby to them, all the same,' I said.

She shook her head. 'It's taboo.' On that point she remained unshaken.

'You can't go back to your husband now. Monster like that is not fit to have a wife. Come and live with me.'

So we started living together. Abunovbo was not a vivacious person, in fact she never recovered from her grief, but she was always pleasant and her calmness made the home a nice place to come to after work. But one day, a man came to my house. His eyes were bloodshot and he carried a matchete in his hand. The first I knew about his visit was when Abunovbo ran to our room with terror in her eyes and fell down at my feet, grasping my ankles.

'Don't let him enter,' she cried.

'Who?' I asked, but she kept on repeating what she had said. I went to the window and looked out. It was then I saw the man with the bloodshot eyes. He came to the house and rapped on the door. I locked the bedroom door before opening the door to him.

'What do you want?' I asked rudely.

'My wife,' he said aggressively.

'This is not the place to look for your wife,' I said and slammed the door in his face.

But when I came back from work the next day, Abunovbo had gone. The furniture in the house had been disturbed and I knew there had been a struggle. For weeks, I made discreet inquiries; for months, I made inquiries that were not so discreet. It wasn't till six months after that I knew where her husband had taken her. So one afternoon I took my car and went there. They lived on the outskirts of the village. As I approached the house I heard the sound of a loud quarrel. Then there were bangs and – silence.

I knocked, but there was no answer. I pushed open the door and entered the house. Abunovbo was sitting on a chair staring at her dead husband, a mallet in her right hand. His skull was fractured. She did not seem surprised to see me.

'I had to kill him,' she said simply. 'He was going to kill our child.' It was then it registered in my mind that she was pregnant – about seven months.

'He said he was going to tear the bastard from my belly. He was holding a barber's razor and came at me with a wicked look on his face. And I knew he meant it. So …' She looked at the mallet in her hand and dropped it.

Despite everything I could do, they brought in a verdict of murder but because she was pregnant, they did not hang her. They sentenced her to life imprisonment instead.

'I'll send you the child,' she whispered to me before she climbed into the Black Maria.

General Ehi

Lieutenant-General Ehi sat in a comfortable overstuffed armchair in a large bed-sitter thinking about many things. It was a well-appointed room with a decor which even he, fastidious as he was, could not find fault with. In other circumstances he would have loved the place. It had been a very large lounge but now, in addition to the overstuffed chairs and the dining-table and chairs, there was a double bed at one end. The upholstery of the lounge chairs picked out the mauve in the pattern of the window blinds that had a cubic design – an unusual decor but with a pleasant effect. In dressing, the general preferred duller colours – beige, brown, grey, but for room decoration he had always preferred something brighter, cheerful. But this time, the cheerful look of the room irritated him. "Too bloody cheerful," he thought to himself. This must be one of their cruel jokes, putting him in this large, pleasant room with no hint of the horror to come.

His mind went back to the last few days but did not dwell on them. For some reason his mind preferred to go beyond the immediate past into the distant past. Could it be because the immediate past was too close to the frightening future for comfort?

The distant past – back in his cadet days. Why had he become a cadet? The uniform, of course. It made you feel important, special. He had always wanted to be special and do the things which most boys were not privileged to do. He had loved everything about the military school, even the tough training and discipline. His friend Kadiri, a cadet too, had once said to him, 'You are a born soldier. You'll go far. You do everything so well and so easily. I have to make a special effort.' That was Kadiri – never jealous, a true friend. They'd shared everything together including their first groping experiences with girls. It had been the same when they met again at the war front during the Civil War. He was a major and Kadiri, a captain. At first Kadiri had behaved stiffly, a bit uneasy about the difference in their ranks. But he had put him at ease immediately and they had resumed their friendship. What a roaring time they'd had at the front. The war front was not what he had expected it to be – a celibate zone where all you thought about was killing the fellows on the other side and avoiding being killed yourself. No, on the contrary, there had been those girls from the other side, boldly trading with the enemy camp, flirting with enemy officers, crossing and re-crossing the battlelines, not caring whom they went with so long as there were rations to be had. One of them had attached herself to Kadiri. Her name was Rose though she was very dark. She had a beautiful skin, though. Kadiri himself was very light-skinned. It was the attraction of opposites.

A frown appeared on his face as he thought of the two. Kadiri and Rose. Strange how other people's actions can impinge on your own life. If those two had not met ... But it was the will of God. It must have been. He must have willed that what they did together would in the end affect him. But he had had no inkling at the time, no inkling.

He heard a sound at the door. A key turned in the lock and the door creaked open. Why don't they oil that door, for God's sake, he wondered irritably. Nothing ever got maintained in the blasted country – like the air conditioner, a good make but rattling away all day, all night. Sometimes he wished it would explode and come crashing down on his head then all his troubles would be over.

The person who had opened the door now came in. He had a gun in his hands which he trained on General Ehi. On the heels of the soldier with the gun – a corporal – came a private carrying a tray of food. The private put the tray on the table. He looked at General Ehi without saluting before he turned to go. General Ehi thought he detected a sneer on the man's face. They say when the big cotton tree falls down, even a child will play on top of it. That private was one of those who used to tremble at the sound of his name.

The corporal with the gun withdrew and carefully locked the door. General Ehi was alone again. He looked at the tray on the table. It was a large table – large enough for a family of eight. The tray with two covered dishes, a finger bowl and a plastic bottle of water looked forlorn in the middle of the table's vastness. A picture of his family rose before him – his wife and their five children. What would his children do without him, especially his two girls who were so fond of him? They thought him a wonderful father. He loved sports and often took them to watch football and polo. He played badminton with them whenever he could. There was a badminton court in front of their house. He wished he had their photograph with him but his wallet had been taken from him. His mind went to his wife. As usual, thinking about her tore him to pieces. Sometimes he loved her with a passion that bordered on obsession, at other times he hated her. He hated her for what she had done to him and what she had made him do. That had been a terrible day. But he must not think about it. He resolutely dragged his mind back to the present.

He rose from the armchair, went to the table and sat on the chair by the tray. He opened one dish. It contained vegetable stew. He opened the other dish. There was *apu* in it – the staple food of his wife's people. He'd met her at the war front and married her at the end of the war. Because he loved her, he had grown to love her people's food. And she was a good cook too. But after that day, that terrible day of betrayal, he had never wanted to eat her type of food again. Now they were serving it to him in his glorified cell. It was all part of their plan to torture him, to drive him out of his senses. He now knew the reason for the rattling air conditioner. He knew all about modern methods of torture, no longer crude but refined, using the intimate knowledge of the victim to break him. How fiendish! With both hands he banged on the covers of the two dishes and was surprised that they did not break. They were pyrex, of course. He would have derived pleasure from the sound of breaking crockery. He rushed to the door and banged on it frantically. The corporal shouted from outside. 'What is the matter?' He shouted back, 'Take the food away! I don't want it. Take it away, I say.' His voice, normally deep, became high-pitched. The corporal shouted, 'Go back to your chair.' He was looking at him through a square glass panel in the door. It would have looked like a hospital door if it had not had bars across it – the only outward sign of his incarceration. The corporal shouted something. A few minutes later, the key turned in the lock and the private who had brought in the food came in. The corporal remained at the door, his gun at the ready. The private looked at the untouched food, then at General Ehi and turned to look questioningly at the corporal. The corporal barked, 'Take the food away, bloody fool. He doesn't want it.' The private quickly lifted the tray from the table and carried it out. In his hurry he collided with the corporal who yelled, 'Look out, bastard!' He locked the door as soon as the private had gone.

Once more peace reigned in the room except for the unnerving rattle of the air conditioner. Once Ehi had turned it off but the heat in the room was unbearable, for all the windows were shut and barred behind the deceptively pleasant blinds. In no time he was sweating. He didn't want to sweat. They'd think he was afraid. He, Ehi? He'd never been afraid of anything in this world; that was what had earned him all his promotions – his bravery. He had received a medal for his exploits during the Civil War and had been mentioned in despatches by the commander of the United Nations peace-keeping force in the Chad. Now he was at the top of his career. His face changed again and wore a bitter look. What top? he asked himself. Some top, he answered himself, cooped up in this claustrophobic, glorified cell and having a mere corporal bark orders at him! Why did the role of the military have to change? Why did they become involved in government? If they hadn't, he would not be here now. So many ifs.

His mind went back to the Civil War. Strange how so many events conspired to change his life so much. If he had not met Kadiri again at the War Front, their friendship would not have become so firmly cemented. Kadiri would have been a vague schoolboy's memory, pleasant to recollect, remaining firmly in its place in the distant past, not intruding into the present. If only Kadiri had not died in the War. Kadiri's death two months before the war came to an end had shattered him. There had been rumours at the time of a vendetta by a jealous lover ditched by the vivacious Rose, of treacherous murder by one of their side. The truth never came out. Ehi had mourned for his friend in the true Nigerian fashion: if only he had left a child, then his lineage would have been perpetuated.

Then one day, long after the war, he had been inspecting a brigade and had come across this fellow who was the spitting image of Kadiri. He nearly gasped with surprise but controlled himself and carried on with the parade, his mind in a whirl. Could it be? No, it couldn't. But it was possible. He made some mental calculations. It was probable. The young man had the same slight upturn of the lips at the left corner of his mouth, the same tall lithe figure, the same light complexion, the same fluffy, slightly curly hair which made you wonder if there was Fulani blood in their family.

After the inspection, he had sent for the young private.

'What is your name?' he asked him.

The young man said, 'Kadiri, sir.'

'Where is your father?'

'He's dead, sir. He died during the Civil War, sir.'

'Was he a soldier?'

'Yes, sir, a captain. Captain Sanni Kadiri.'

General Ehi could not help exclaiming, 'But he was not married!'

The young man smiled a rather charming lopsided smile, the type that sent women's hearts fluttering. He said, 'He wasn't, sir, but he had a son. He met my mother in the East during the war. Her name was Rose.'

'Was?'

'She's dead, sir. She died of infective hepatitis. You know how it raged after the war. She told me all about my father.'

General Ehi remembered the epidemic too well. The war

damage had broken down the water supply system and in the poor unhygienic conditions where streams and bushes became natural toilets, it was easy for an epidemic to spread. Ehi's first thought was to thank God that Kadiri did not die without a son. His second thought was that young Kadiri was an orphan. He felt an obligation towards his best friend's son. He must help him. He must care for him. He made him his batman. It was the most he could do for his friend's son who did not have much education.

Chukwu Kadiri turned out to be the best batman General Ehi ever had. He did his work very cheerfully and got on well with his children. He did not even mind washing his wife's clothes and sometimes the children's. This delighted his wife who had often grumbled that 'these batmen think they're to serve only you.' He felt very affectionate towards young Kadiri and often told him stories about his father and himself during the war. He treated him more like a son than a batman. His children, too, regarded Chukwu as an elder brother and played games with him in the compound.

But one day his wife came to him and said, 'I think you should change your batman.' He was astounded. To him, young Kadiri was the perfect batman. He knew he was often away on both military and state duties and he did not need to take his batman with him, especially as he was a member of the Supreme Redemption Council. Could young Kadiri be a sort of Dr. Jekyl-and-Mr-Hyde character, behaving well in his presence and misbehaving when he wasn't there?

'Why?' he demanded.

His wife was silent.

'Has he been rude to you?'

'No, he's always polite.'

'Does he ill-treat the children?'

'No'

'Then why? Why change him? You have no complaints against him.'

His wife spoke, at first hesitatingly, 'Well – you see – er – you know the girls are growing up. They're becoming young women. Chukwu is very handsome. I don't want anything developing between them.'

'That's rubbish,' Ehi had pronounced. 'Young Kadiri is a well-behaved boy. He knows why I took him on. He wouldn't let down his father's memory.'

But he had had to get rid of young Kadiri in the end. It had been very painful but he had had no alternative after his shock discovery. Honour demanded it. His replacement was not a patch on young Kadiri. In fact he irritated him with his servile attitude and jumping to attention on all occasions. His presence reminded him of young Kadiri's absence. He missed young Kadiri who was always polite, but never servile.

Ehi's pre-occupation with the coup plan had helped him to shut young Kadiri from his mind. Looking back now, he realized it was a mad plan. Whoever heard of staging a coup by getting foreign mercenaries to invade the country and install him as Head of State? He had taken advantage of his position as Minister of Internal Affairs to let them into the country. He had hidden the advance party in an out-of-the-way camp from where they would emerge when the time was ripe and strike on land, while their colleagues mounted an air attack. In a way he was going to wage war against his country but the end justifies the means. He had his dreams for the country.

Now those dreams would never be fulfilled. Someone had noticed the presence of aliens in the area of the camp and his mercenaries had been picked up even before any blow had been struck. That was the bitter part. What on earth could have pushed him to embark on such a mad ambitious plan, his friends wondered. He had everything – money, prestige, a beautiful wife and five fine children who were doing well at school and at university. How were they to know that there was an emptiness in him that needed to be filled? Having lost those things that were dearest to him on that unforgettable day, was it not logical that he should want to replace that terrible loss with something? How were they to know that something stronger than himself was egging him on, some inexorable urge that was pushing him to his doom? He was beginning to suspect whose invisible hand was directing his affairs. He had dreamt again last night – the same dream he had dreamt since they put him under house arrest. In the dream a sorrowful Kadiri – the elder Kadiri – had appeared to him and said, 'Could you not have forgiven him for my sake? It wasn't all his fault, you know.' As usual, he had woken up in a sweat. He had looked towards the peephole to see if the guard was watching him. The light switch was outside and he could not turn off the light so his guards could always see what he was doing. There was no face at the window. But he sensed a presence in the room. He looked round but there was nobody in the room with him. Then he heard a whisper, 'Master, she invited me.'

He knew that voice. It had said something he had not wanted to admit to himself. Before, he had been praying for a reprieve. He was still in his prime. But now he knew he no longer wanted to live. There was nothing to live for. Part of him had died that day when all was revealed and he had had to take that terrible final action. The rest had died when they came to arrest him, not for that first action which he had covered up so well but for his non-action. He'd like to die now. He'd like to join young Kadiri and his father and ask them to forgive him. He buried his head in his hands.

He was in this position when the soldiers came to take him to the stake. He looked up and got a shock. Their leader was young Kadiri, not whining and pleading in vain for mercy that time Ehi had pointed his loaded gun at him as he cowered on the bed beside his master's wife, completely naked. This was a masterful Chukwu Kadiri, dressed inexplicably in his father's uniform, a triumphant look on his face. 'Sir, you are to come with us.'

So this was where Fate was leading him. He did not mind. There was nothing to live for, anyway. He got up and shouted, 'I'm coming, Kadiri, I'm coming to join you!' Then he fell down just as young Kadiri had fallen after he shot him in the heat of betrayal. Captain Uyo, the leader of the team, stepped into the room and stooped over the fallen general. He knelt on one knee and put his ear to the general's heart. After some time he got up. Turning to the armed group behind him, he said, 'This one has beaten the stake.'

'What was that about Kadiri? Who's Kadiri?' one of the soldiers said.

The leader shrugged, 'Dunno,' he said. 'It doesn't matter anyway.'

The Mat

The lorry came to where a sign said, 'OKI, DRIVE SLOWLY', but did not slow down. It dashed into the town scattering fowls, goats and children right and left, and continued on its mad career till it reached the market. It was market day and the market was full. The lorry discharged some passengers and went further into the town. At two points it stopped and some more passengers got down. One of the lorry boys turned to an old woman sitting on the middle bench, 'Didn't you say you were getting down at Oki?'

'Yes,' she replied in a harsh voice.

'Well, this is Oki,' the lorry boy said. 'Where do you want us to put you down?'

'At my daughter's,' she replied.

'Your daughter's? But …'

'My daughter Aina,' she said, as if clarifying matters still more.

'But where does she live?' the second lorry boy asked.

'I don't know.'

'Well, what are we going to do now?' the first boy asked.

'I vote we dump her somewhere and go our way. We've still a long way to go.'

The woman let out a stream of curses: 'If you dare do that and I lose my way, may Heaven punish you, you …'

'Old Mother,' one of the passengers, a mild-looking youth in a khaki travelling suit tried to remonstrate with her. She turned a baleful eye on him and he kept quiet.

The lorry boys conferred. They were afraid to offend an old woman with one foot in the grave. If she were to curse them … The lorry driver, impatient and not knowing what was happening, called out to ask what was keeping them from moving. The second lorry boy went to the front part of the lorry and told him.

'We'll go back to the market and ask people where the girl lives,' he said.

So they went back to the market. They approached a woman selling yams and asked her if she knew Aina. She told them she did not live in the town but had come to the market from a neighbouring village. They tried two more people and they did not know either. They were turning to go to another part of the market, thinking the part they were in was reserved for strangers, when a tailor came out from his stall and asked, 'Are you looking for someone?'

'Yes, my daughter Aina,' the old woman answered.

'Is she married?'

'Yes, her husband's name is Ogun.'

'What work does he do?'

'He's a shoemaker.'

'Oh, I know him. Akande!' he called to one of his apprentices. 'Come and take these people to the shoemaker's house.'

The boy came out of the shed and they all got onto the lorry.

Between her two-roomed house and the kitchen hut Aina was pounding yam. She was tall and strongly built and, though she was expecting a baby, she did not appear to find the work difficult. She was putting the finishing touches to the yam, rolling it round and round in the mortar and glazing it with water when she heard voices and two people came round the corner of the house.

'Mother!' she cried. She abandoned the long pestle and went to embrace her mother. The pestle bounced out of the mortar and fell on the ground carrying some of the yam with it. Aina turned back as she heard the clatter and pouted.

'Now I shan't have any to eat,' she said. 'It will just be enough for my husband and you.'

'Nonsense,' said her mother. 'You've got to eat well in your state. You can make Ogun some eba.'

She turned and saw that the tailor's boy was still waiting.

'Waiting for a tip, eh?' she said in a nasty tone.

The boy disappeared quickly.

The Mat

'These children are all rogues,' Aina's mother said, 'can't do anything without expecting a reward.'

Aina led her mother inside the house and came back to remove the yam from the mortar.

Ogun was singing blithely on his way home. He was a small, nondescript man with a weak mouth and very coarse work-worn hands, calloused and scarred all over. His face normally wore a cheerful expression but today he had a special reason for being cheerful. Business had been good. Two chiefs had commissioned two pairs of carpet slippers each and several debtors had paid him what they owed. As he came near his house his singing changed to whistling. At the door he called 'Aina.'

Aina's mother came to the door.

'Oh', he said, taken aback, 'We didn't know you were coming!'

'I don't have to ask permission before I visit my own daughter, do I?' she retorted.

'I didn't mean it that way.' Ogun said weakly.

'How did you mean it?' she asked dangerously.

Ogun was saved from answering by the appearance of his wife; she was holding a big rolled up mat in her right hand.

'Look what mother brought,' she announced, 'isn't it beautiful?'

She held the mat at one edge and let the rest fall towards the ground. A beautiful sight met their eyes. It was a specially woven mat, with a village scene depicted on it in brilliant colours.

Ogun did not know what to think. There was the woman quarrelling with him as soon as she saw him and here was this beautiful present. Perhaps behind her rough manners she was really kind. The mat must have been specially ordered.

'Thank you, Mother,' he said. 'Have you eaten?' His mother-in-law said that she had eaten. 'But there is one thing that pains me,' she added. 'When I arrived I found Aina pounding yam. In her condition, too! I won't have my daughter overworking herself. After all it's your child she's carrying. Her father always did the rough work whenever I was pregnant. I'm glad I came after all to take care of my daughter. I shall stay on till the child begins to walk.'

That evening they talked far into the night with Aina asking questions about home and her mother telling her all the gossip. At last Ogun got up. He went out to the latrine preparatory to going to bed. When he finished he saw his neighbour, Odedina, and they fell to talking. They talked for a long time and at last Ogun said goodnight and entered his house. He found his mother-in-law firmly ensconced on his bed with her daughter beside her.

He now understood about the mat.

The following morning, he was roused by a sharp tap on the body followed by a shake. He rolled over sleepily and asked 'Whatisit?'

'Get up and split the wood,' his mother-in-law said, 'I won't have my daughter breaking wood in her condition.'

Ogun rose and broke the wood, then fetched water from the stream and made the fire.

And that was only the beginning. Aina's mother firmly took charge of the household. She saw to it that things were done her own way. And Aina, for her part, now that Ogun's imperfections were pointed out to her, began to wonder how she could have borne such hardships for so long. She became mulish and spoilt and would not bestir herself in the house. Ogun went on breaking wood, fetching water and pounding yam. And as Aina grew rounder so did her fondness for pounded yam increase, and Ogun found himself pounding yam every afternoon. This made him so tired that sometimes he fell asleep over his shoemaking.

When Ogun complained to people they said, 'why don't you beat her?' He explained, 'You see, whenever I try to beat Aina her mother always interposes herself and says if I beat her daughter I've got to beat her too. And I can't beat an old woman like that. Suppose she were to die. I'd be in trouble.' So people stopped advising him to beat his wife.

Things came to a head one day. It was very near a festival

The Mat

and Ogun had been very busy trying to get some shoes finished. One or two children had come to his shop and burst into tears because their sandalets were not ready. Two women passing by thought he had beaten them and scolded him severely. Then many people had come railing on him to finish their shoes. Ogun worked very hard and got them all finished. Then he got ready to go home. He had had no lunch and he felt very, very tired. With dragging steps he went homewards and the first words that greeted him were 'Why were you not home at lunch-time?' from his wife and 'you good-for-nothing, been sleeping again in your shop and pretending to work, eh?' from his mother-in-law.

Ogun controlled his temper.

'The yam is just done,' his wife said, 'we had to eat *eba* for lunch because you didn't come.'

'I'm not going to pound yam tonight; I'm tired!'

His mother-in-law said calmly, 'You won't enter the house till you've pounded the yam.' She and her daughter stood guarding the back door. For one mad moment Ogun thought of pushing them both out of the way. Then commonsense asserted itself. His mother-in-law would yell that he'd been murdering her and probably die to spite him. But where to sleep? He pondered over this for some time. Then he decided to go to his cousin on the other side of town. He was a bachelor and could easily put him up.

His cousin was a little out of patience with him. 'Beat the old woman and damn the consequences,' he counselled.

But Ogun was not made of such stern stuff. 'It's taboo, you know, to touch one's mother-in-law.'

'Well, run away, then, if you can't be a man,' his cousin said in disgust and returned to bed.

The following day Ogun returned home and found his wife and her mother talking. They did not see him as he stood by the window. He overheard his mother-in-law saying, 'I'm going to see a *juju* man tomorrow. I must do something about that good-for-nothing husband of yours.'

Ogun became frightened. She might put a potion in his

soup to stupefy him and make him do whatever she asked. Such potions had been known to kill inadvertently. He fled to his shop. In the shop he found himself remembering his cousin's words. 'Well, run away then,' he had said. Why not? he thought. He packed his tools and left the town.

At the next village he stopped, found himself a shop, set out his tools and awaited customers. None came. So he decided to go from house to house and introduce himself. The first day he got one commission, the second day the village shoemaker came to him with a group of friends and told him with suitably impressive threats to clear out, the place was not big enough for two shoemakers. He stuck it out for a month, then packed his tools and left.

Aina's mother was sitting gazing out of the window one evening when she saw a dusty figure at a distance.

'There is that good-for-nothing husband of yours coming back,' she called to her daughter.

Aina came to the window, 'So it is. It's lucky I decided not to break the wood before tomorrow morning.'

'Don't talk to him,' her mother said.

The figure came nearer. He entered the house and said 'E ku'le.' No one answered. He put some *gari* in a bowl and added water. Still no one spoke. When he finished eating, he looked round. 'Will no one speak to me?' he asked.

'There's some wood in the backyard,' his mother-in-law said. He went out and broke the wood.

In the evening he asked 'where is my mat?'

'It's gone,' his wife said.

'Gone?' he asked.

'We've sold it. We had to sell many things. You didn't leave us any money, you know.'

'Where is the old mat?' he asked his wife.

'It's under the mattress and we can't get up.'

Ogun went to the kitchen, brought out a soiled and tattered mat and spread it on the parlour floor. Then he curled up on it and slept.

'Who Will Bury Me?'

If you go to the village of Omini in the midwestern part of Nigeria, as you enter the village from the east side you will see a house a little distance away from the rest. It has a motled, leprous look with the paint flaking off in most places, the iron sheets of the roof rusty and leaking. There are neither doors nor windows and so without any effort at all you can see the floor inside, an undulating eyesore of mud and crumbling cement. In short, the house is in a shocking state of disrepair. Not that anyone would ever want to repair it, for the house has *juju*. Not one will go near it. Children, coming home late from fetching firewood, glance uneasily at it and whisper fearfully as they hurry past, wondering if they will see the ghost of the old woman.

The old woman was not old when she first came to live in the village. She came one evening from a neighbouring town, a young and beautiful bride, with expressive eyes and dimpled cheeks. She arrived in a heavy downpour and everybody said what a lucky bride Onotoe was and how fruitful she was going to be. The ceremonial washing of her feet on the threshold seemed hardly necessary after nature's more lavish ceremony.

She soon settled into the life of the village. Her husband Imana was several years older and treated her with that kindly indulgence which only a man of maturer years can display. They lived contentedly, he going to his farm, she working at her hand loom.

Nor did she belie the prophesy of the villagers. Not quite a year after her marriage she had a son. The son looked neither like tiny Onotoe nor did he bear any resemblance to tall and willowy Imana. He never had that wobbly fat baby look which most children have. Instead he had strong, sturdy limbs, a muscular body and a face that already looked older than his age. He was not a monster – far from it – but an unusual sort of child. Everybody said what a useful help-mate he was going to be on Imana's farm. Imana himself proudly went about saying it was his grandfather come back to life.

'He's just like my granpa,' he would say. 'You didn't know him? He was the strongest man in his time – and my son Akintunde is just the spit of him. A-kin-tun-de – the Brave One has returned.'

Two years later Onotoe had another son and thereafter she had a son every other year. Altogether there were seven children – all boys.

'I envy you your old age,' one of Imana's friends would say, as they sat down playing *ayo* and drinking palm wine. 'With seven sons to watch over your old age, all you have to do is sit back and reap the fruits of your labour.'

'What labour?' an old woman would scream, for old women have no modesty. 'What had he to do with it? It's the woman who bears the whole burden.'

Imana would laugh 'And quite rightly too. Divine Providence is so wise – and just,' he would say with a twinkle in his eye. He was a popular man in the village as all who joke and play *ayo* must be.

Onotoe herself felt very proud of her seven sons. In the evening they would gather round her while she told them moonlight stories. They learnt how the tortoise's shell became so rough, how people came to have the groove running down their backs and many other things that are only told in the evenings. Imana's farm prospered and soon he had two more outside the town.

Then suddenly tragedy struck. Akintunde, the eldest son went one day with his father and Agbadia, the brother next to him, to one of the distant farms. It had been a very hot day and the three farmers sat down under the shade of a tree to rest. Agbadia went to the fire which they had made in the open and brought out a roasted yam. He took it to his father who divided it into three. Akintunde cut a piece out of his own share and was about to eat it when something fell on his head from the tree. It ran quickly round his neck forming a giant necklace. Horrified, the other two watched. Akintunde himself was petrified. The younger brother made to put his hand towards the snake but his father restrained him 'Don't move,' he told Akintunde. The snake looked at them dully, its forked tongue sticking out of its mouth. Then it began slowly to unwind itself, travelling downwards with a slow movement. The watchers were about to heave a sigh of relief when a twig fell from the tree right on to the head of the snake. Shocked, the snake curved itself back and struck Akintunde right on the chest.

And that was how Imana's firstborn died. Everybody sympathised with him and said what a pity but he was still better off than most; he had six sons still. Imana smiled ruefully and agreed with them.

But that was only the beginning. The following year the second son went swimming and drowned. The year after that a third son fell from a palm tree and split his head open.

People said Onotoe was a witch. The thought went round the village first as only the ghost of a suggestion, then it grew into a loud and insistent rumour, from which it reached the final stage of unshakeable conviction. If Imana had had a mother she would have been the witch, if he had had a second wife she would have been the witch, but in the absence of these two favourite culprits, Onotoe had to serve.

At first a few friends stuck by her and asked her detractors what reasons she could possibly have for killing her own children. But the latter had their argument. Some women, they said, sold their children to the devil for money – a suggestion which was borne out by the fact that she made a great deal of money from her woven cloth trade. Onotoe must take the Witch Test, they said.

At first Imana would not listen to this suggestion. But his friends went on at him. 'How old are you now?' they asked and when he said 'fifty rains' they said, 'You see, there are all your children dying before your very eyes and by the time you think of doing something about it it will be too late. Better do something now.'

And so it was decided that Onotoe should take the Witch Test. There was quite a ceremony about it. Imana and his friends and some very old men and women of the village sat in a semi-circle and watched Onotoe drink the poisonous mixture. If she was a witch she would die. Slowly, Onotoe drank the poison. At first nothing happened. Then she clutched at her stomach and bent double. She retched and retched and retched, and then vomited. But she did not die. There was great rejoicing in Imana's house that night, especially among the remaining children who had not liked the idea of their mother being a witch.

But the following morning one of them did not get up from his mat.

Fear entered into the heart of everybody. This was powerful witchcraft from another town. How to deal with it? Half-crazed, Imana went to his friends for advice. 'You take another wife – this time from among us,' they said, 'and start afresh. Consider you have no family now. That is the best thing.'

So Imana started courting Osen, a girl of twenty whom he had known from her childhood. But an unexpected difficulty arose.

'I can't live with that witch,' Osen said.

'I'll send her away, then,' Imana said.

'That won't do,' Osen still objected, 'I won't live in that cursed house.'

So he and Osen went to live in his farmhouse until he should have built another house in the town. Left with the children, Onotoe wept bitter tears but in the end took heart and, calling her children together, said, 'I have no husband now, and you children have no father. But do not despair. You will live to bury me.'

Vain hope. Not long after, one of the children mistakenly ate a toadstool and died. Onotoe called the remaining two children together: 'You'll live to bury me, won't you?' It was a desperate appeal this time. When there was only the youngest remaining she said, 'You, at least, my dearest, will be spared to bury me.'

And it seemed as if her wishes would be fulfilled. For years the two of them lived together happily, living on the proceeds from the nearby farm which Imana had left to them. Onotoe was now growing old and depending more and more on her son, a gentle youth who looked very much like his father.

Then one day Dele came to his mother and said, 'I want to marry.' His mother was delighted.

'Have you anybody in mind?'

'Yes, mother. Ebun is a very beautiful girl. And well-behaved. You know her – Bankole's daughter.'

'Do you want me to speak to her father?'

'Not yet, but I want you to sound her first. I've never spoken to her before.'

But when Onotoe spoke to Ebun she laughed and said, 'No fear, I don't want to be cursed too.'

Weeping in her heart for her son, Onotoe sat in her kitchen wondering what lie to tell him. He came back from the farm and stood at the door, a tall, lanky figure. He looked so young and defenceless.

'What did she say?' he asked.

His mother struggled for words, 'She ... she ...' and then burst into tears despite herself.

'I know,' he said and went into the house, put some clothes in a bundle and started walking away. His mother ran after him, shouting, 'Where are you going? Who will bury me? Come back.'

She caught up with him and grabbed him by the arm. He shook off her hands roughly and said, 'Leave me alone, you witch.'

She stood stock still, shocked, then watched him as his figure receded into the distance.

The old woman was now alone. Her life became mechanical. She lived because there was nothing else to do. Bowed down with mental suffering, she began to suffer in health. Once she fell seriously ill and as she lay staring at the ceiling one night, a panic thought came to her – suppose she should die, who would bury her? Would they make a coffin for her? She couldn't lie still in her grave without a coffin. The thought became an obsession. 'There's no one to bury me properly, there's no one to bury me properly,' ran the perpetual refrain in her mind.

So when she got well she had a coffin made. When the carpenter brought it to her, she asked him if the wood was strong. He said, yes, of course, he never did inferior work. She did not see the sly, conspiratorial wink which the carpenter gave his mate, nor the mate's answering grin. 'I can now rest in my grave,' she declared. Her health failed rapidly. She grew poor and could scarcely move from the house. All her clothes were tattered. Then there came the worst rains the village had ever experienced. It rained for weeks at a time. The doors and windows of the house fell into disrepair and one by one they were yanked off their hinges and thrown outside to rot in the rain. Weak with hunger and cold the old woman could now hardly leave her mat. One bitterly cold night she tottered towards the coffin and lay down in it. It was quite warm.

'And if I die,' she thought, 'all the better.'

It was the stormiest night of the season. The wind howled through the trees and the rain was like a whiplash. The crash of falling trees combined with the crash of thunder to create a tremendous din and occasionally there was a series of lightning flashes which rendered the gloom even more oppressive afterwards. Far away in the next town a convict took the opportunity which the inclement weather provided to break out of gaol. Armed with a matchete, a box of matches and a couple of cigarettes, he proceeded towards the next town. The weather which had been his friend now turned his enemy. Battling his way through, soaked to the skin, and with his teeth chattering, he came to the old woman's house. A momentary flash lit up the doorway and he dashed in. He could not see anything. He fumbled in his pockets and brought out the box of matches. The next few moments were punctuated by the 'phut' sound of matches being struck against a damp box. At last he got some light. He looked round him. A lot of dried *eko* leaves and oily rags were strewn all over the floor. An axe

'Who Will Bury Me?'

stood behind the door leading to the backyard and beside it on the floor was a smooth, crooked stick which had probably served as a walking-stick. He picked up the stick, wrapped a rag round one end and put it in the fire until it glowed and burst into flames. Using the stick as a torch, he went into a room to his right to see if he could find some furniture to put on the fire. The only item of furniture was a coffin. He peered into the coffin and encountered the lack lustre gaze of the old woman. Suddenly her eyes flickered and her lips began to move. 'Oh my son, my dear son,' she whispered, 'you have come back to bury me.' She closed her eyes and subsided into the coffin, a slight smile on her lips as if she had found contentment at last. The convict looked at her for a few seconds, then quickly dug out the corpse from the coffin and threw it on the floor like an old rag doll. He carried the coffin back to the dying fire and began feverishly to split the wood with the axe. He really must hurry, he thought, or he would die of cold. At last he got three splinters and put them on the fire. They began to smoulder.

The convict sat back to rest.

Ahimie's Wives

When Ahimie saw that the sheet on his bed had been changed for the third time in one day, he knew he was in for trouble. He had three wives the eldest of whom had five children and no longer slept with him. The second wife had one child, while the third was childless. Both were always competing for his attentions. Each one spread her own sheet, usually made of patterned Dutch wax print, on the bed whenever it was her turn 'to sleep.' But sometimes the roster arrangement was disrupted as the wives believed that the period immediately after their menstrual flow was their most fertile period. Then the wife who had just become 'clean' would insist on sleeping with her husband that night.

It had been a long, hard day for Ahimie who worked in the public works department as he had had to stand in the sun for hours supervising repairs to a stretch of road which had been damaged by the heavy rains of the previous season. He was close to retirement and looking forward to a deserved rest after working for thirty-five years, but what about these women who would give him no peace? He wished it were possible to retire from matrimonial obligations.

At this point in his thoughts, Third Wife entered the room, whipped off the cloth on the bed and spread another on it. Second wife came in, noticed the new cloth and, in turn, whipped it off the bed. Third Wife flew at her and a struggle ensued. Their husband commanded, 'Stop it! Stop it! Stop it, I say.'

Second Wife stopped because she was not so desperate but the childless wife now started spreading her cloth back on the bed. Ahimie shouted at her: 'Take it off and get out. Get out, both of you. I don't want either of you tonight. Get OUT!'

Second Wife went out but hovered by the door. Third Wife, however, paid no heed and continued spreading her cloth.

Her husband said, 'If you don't remove that cloth immediately I shall beat you.'

The woman continued with what she was doing. Her husband took off a slipper and whacked her on the back. She turned and faced him and he started pushing her out of the room, at the same time beating her with the slipper. Third Wife began to howl and the neighbours came round to see what the commotion was all about. Ahimie managed to push her out. He was going back inside when she grabbed his big white sleeping cloth which he had thrown casually over the left shoulder. Second Wife tried to pull her off. The movement caught him unawares and he tripped over the open drain running along the foot of the wall. He fell heavily on his back.

First Wife who had stood outside shouting to Third Wife to stop fighting with their husband, now rushed to his aid but a neighbour who happened to be a nurse told her to leave him alone until a doctor could be summoned.

The doctor came and examined Ahimie. He took Ahimie's first wife aside and said, 'I think your husband has suffered a severe back injury. He cannot move his lower limbs and I suspect he is paralysed from the waist down. I'll have him taken into hospital.'

First Wife set up a loud wail. 'See what you have done, see what you have done, both of you!' she railed at the other wives as the doctor made arrangements to hospitalize Ahimie.

Hospital tests revealed an irreparable spinal injury and Ahimie remained paralysed from the waist down. When he came back to the house, his conscience-stricken wives expected him to be angry with them and perhaps send them back to their homes. But Ahimie was not angry. He was always one to count his blessings. Of late he had been finding it hard to arouse himself to fulfil his marital obligations. Now he need not bother anymore, ever again.

The Confidante

I was just leaving the cocktail party when someone introduced us. I'd seen her several times before and the intense expression on her face, the haunted look in her eyes, had always aroused my curiosity so I said, 'I've always wanted to meet you. I've seen you several times before, you know.'

She gave me a piercing look and said, 'Where?' with some intensity. I could see it was not just the conventional question of a bored cocktail acquaintance. She really wanted to know.

'Oh, here and there, you know. In front of the post office, at the bank …'

She said, cutting in abruptly, 'Why don't you come to my place Wednesday evening – eightish. Come to dinner. I'm having a few people in.'

As she said this she gripped me by my left wrist. It was a frightening grip – so intense, so impatient, so urgent that I couldn't help wondering if she was a maniac of some sort. If she had been a man I would have imagined I was going to be assaulted.

Mumbling a hasty acceptance I freed my wrist from her grip and fled down the drive, her small, birdlike eyes boring into my back. I decided I wasn't going to the dinner on Wednesday. In any case I did not know where she lived. But the next day I received a note from her together with her visiting card. How did she know where to find me? I wondered. It must have been curiosity that made me change my mind. A quarter to nine on Wednesday found me on her doorstep, drawn there by some irresistible force. As soon as I knocked she opened the door.

'Come in, dear,' she said, holding the door open. She was wearing a long white evening dress which made her look like the high priestess of some ancient cult, and there was an air of excitement about her.

I entered and found myself in a dining-cum-sitting room that was sparsely furnished.

'Sit down, dear,' she said, indicating an armchair that was leaning against a long window. She herself sat on a pouffe at my feet.

I said, 'I thought I would be the last to arrive. I had some difficulty finding this place.'

She gave me a strange look.

'There are no other guests if that's what you want to know,' she said.

I wanted to ask her why there were no other guests when she had specifically said the opposite when she invited me, but I was tongue-tied, overwhelmed by the mystery about her. 'Why doesn't she sit down in a chair?' I thought irritably. Her sitting on that pouffe in front of me made me feel uncomfortable. It was such an intimate position, one that was not justified by our slight acquaintance. Serves me right, I thought, coming to dinner in a stranger's house.

Her voice cut into my thoughts.

'I chose you,' she intoned in a faraway voice, 'I chose you because I knew you would understand.'

I did not know what to say to this and opened and closed my handbag in an involuntary gesture of embarrassment.

'You see,' she went on, 'I had to tell somebody and I knew you would understand. As soon as I saw you I knew you would understand.'

She was repeating the phrase as if to convince herself that it really was so.

'I'll tell you the story from the beginning,' she began.

'Don't you think you'll be more comfortable in a chair?' I said to her, as if I was the hostess and she my guest. You see, her nearness was searing into me.

She shook her head and continued to sit on the pouffe, her knees nearly touching mine. She began her story.

'I was very young when I got married. I'd just left college, in fact. My husband's people did not like me and the more I tried to win them over the farther they receded. They were mostly illiterates, you see, and resented the way my husband treated me as an equal. My husband and I were happy together except for the occasions on which we had to visit his people. Then it was misery being among them, knowing their feelings about me. But one of them was different. She was only a little older than me and she'd had some education. She would come into our room and chat with me. Sometimes she even bought me fabrics so that we could both wear the same outfit at family ceremonies. But what was she among so many? I did not really care for family uniforms but I felt grateful and tried to repay her kindness.

'When my babies began to arrive she was most helpful and would come to stay with me, bathing them and mixing their feeds. But usually I didn't need her help for long; the babies all died within a few weeks. One minute they would be playing, another and they would be gone – without warning.

'After three had died without cause I grew desperate.' She paused and looked into my face.

'You won't call me a murderer if I tell you the next bit?' she asked. I was shocked.

'I ... I ...' I began.

'No,' she answered for me. 'I knew you would understand.'

That phrase was getting on my nerves. I felt she was making me an accessory to an act I was not even aware of. But I had to listen.

'Soon after my third child died,' she continued, 'I began to expect another one. You can imagine my feelings then – uncertainty, dread. I was overwhelmed by the futility of it all. To make matters worse my husband's attitude to me was now changing. His relations had seized on my misfortune to try to do away with someone they had never liked. Take another wife, they kept saying to him. He didn't but the situation made him unhappy. He became unapproachable, especially after visits to his people.

'I knew things could not continue the way they were. If my next child should die, my husband might collapse beneath the weight of his people's arguments. What was I to do?

'A friend of mine told me about a medicine-man and in desperation I went to him. He told me one of my husband's people was a witch and had been responsible for my misfortune.

"Go home," he said, "and write a list of all your husband's female relatives. Omit nobody. Bring the list to me tomorrow evening together with a small goat, three bottles of palm-oil, seven kolanuts and a bottle of gin. We must make a sacrifice. Then we shall know the wicked one. We shall deal with her."

'You can imagine my excitement. As soon as I got home I started on the list. I was tempted to omit my friend's name but the man had said, omit nobody. So I included her name. I had just folded the list when my husband entered my bedroom. I hastily thrust the paper out of sight.

"I only came to say I'm going out and won't want supper," he said and momentarily my heart sank. He'd taken to going out every evening and staying out late.

"All right," I said, cheering myself with the thought that soon things would be all right again.

'Next evening I could not leave the house early because of visitors and when I was ready to go I could not find the list. I thought I might have put it in the drawer of my dressing table in my haste to conceal it but it was not there. I tore another sheet from my writing pad and drew up another list, numbering it as I had been told. The goat and other things were in a friend's house and I hurried out to collect them.

'I got to the medicine-man's house long after the street lights had been turned on.

"You're late," he said. I explained to him what had happened. He took the goat into an inner chamber and I followed him in. I was a little frightened to see the paraphernalia of his calling – the cowrie shells, the medicine containers hung up on one wall, blood-stained feathers on the opposite wall, and in the middle of the room, facing the door a diminutive carved figure with bulbous eyes which stared disconcertingly at the visitor. I sat down on a low stool and kept my eyes down.

'The medicine-man asked for my list and I took it out of my bag.'

"Keep it," he said, "but read out the names in the order in which they were written."

'As I read out each name he made a symbol with charcoal on the floor some distance from the carving. When the names had all been called he laid hold on the goat and slaughtered it with a long, sharp knife. As the blood gushed out I felt sick. Hastily I took out some tissues from my bag.

'The medicine-man sprinkled some of the blood on the carving, then took some of the oil and smeared it on it. The kolanuts he split up and spread in the pool of blood on the ground. He then began an impassioned incantation at the end of which he was panting. For some time he gazed fixedly at the symbols he had made on the ground, then began to stab at each one in turn, pausing slightly at each stab. Nothing happened. Suddenly as he stabbed at the eighteenth symbol a yelping sound came from the wall behind the carved figure.

"That's the evil-doer," the man said triumphantly. "Now let's check from your list."

'I began to look in my bag but he said, "that's it over there," pointing to the ground beside me. I looked and the list was there. I was a bit puzzled because I thought I'd returned it to my bag. Nevertheless I picked it up and looked for the eighteenth name and then I got the shock of my life. It was my friend – the only one among them who had shown me any consideration.

"But – but that's my friend among them all," I protested, my heart beating wildly.

"My *juju* never errs, trust no friends," the man replied – "Friends are more dangerous than enemies because they have access to one's belongings. Does this your friend come to your house?"

I had to admit this and he said, "There you are."

"What am I to do then?" I asked in a daze.

"She must be got rid of," he replied.

"How?" I asked, fear entering my heart.

"She must die."

"But I can't do such a thing," I said.

"If she doesn't die she will surely kill you – if your husband does not send you away. Meanwhile your children will keep on dying. You will always have *abikus*."

"Oh God, Oh God," I moaned.

"It is either you or she. Choose."

"I'm not going to do it," I said and rose.

'He shrugged and I left. When I got home my husband was out as usual. As I sat in my room thinking, the child in my womb stirred and I suddenly saw the implication of my squeamishness. I saw again the tiny lifeless bodies that had to be shut up in the little wooden boxes. I saw a procession of these little boxes stretching "till the crack of doom" – my doom!'

'This child at least, I decided, must be given a chance to live. That same night I went back to the medicine-man.

"I thought you would return," he said, smiling. "I have prepared the medicine for you. Put it in her *eko* as soon as you have the chance."

'I took the packet away and did as I'd been told.'

She broke off, noticing my horrified expression. 'I had to do it, don't you see? I had to. It was self-defence. It was either me or her and I'd suffered enough.'

Her voice was jerky. She leaned forward and gripped me by the arms, hemming me in the chair. Again I had that experience as of one about to be assaulted.

'You understand, don't you? I had no. I had to.' Her voice rose to a scream and her face was all puckered up.

'You had to,' I repeated.

She didn't seem to be quite gratified by this. Perhaps it was because I had echoed her words and this somehow gave a tinge of irony to them. Nevertheless she went on.

'One of the things I had dreaded was having to go to her funeral. But I was spared that – by Fate.'

She smiled a bitter smile. She wasn't gripping me now but she had picked up a handkerchief and was twisting it round her fingers.

'I fell ill, very ill, and couldn't leave my bed. Everybody was wonderful and said I must have been prostrated by my friend's death. And so I was – if only they knew the reason!'

She paused and looked into my face. 'I lost the child, after all,' she said simply. 'Miscarriage.' Her next words came slowly, as if in resignation to Fate.

'My husband too. Brought in another wife one evening without a word to me. There was no fight, no quarrel. They simply behaved as if I wasn't there. I had to go. I began to pack my things. One day, as I was emptying my handbag – it hadn't been emptied for months and contained a lot of junk – lipstick, powder compact, receipts, shopping lists – all the usual sort of things. I was emptying the bag of all these things when the list I had taken to the medicine-man fluttered to the floor. I picked it up and was about to tear it to pieces when a second list caught my attention. It was jutting out of the bag. I drew it out. Two lists. So they had both been in the bag! When had the first list got into the bag? And then in a flash I saw the whole thing. When my husband had come into my room I'd hidden the list. I thought I'd put it in the chest of drawers but had not found it there when I looked. I must have put the list in my bag which was open beside me. Not finding the list, I'd written a second list and put it in the bag. I'd presented the second list to the medicine-man and he'd put down his symbols according to the order on that list. Then he had performed the sacrifice and asked for the list again. It was found on the floor though I had a feeling I'd returned it to the bag. I was a little puzzled at the time but now I knew. When I'd taken out the tissues because I felt sick the first list which I'd mislaid had fluttered out of it without my knowing.'

'I was horrified. Could it be ...? Oh God, pray it isn't. It mustn't ... But it was. I checked the two lists and the order of names was different. Number eighteen on the second list was someone else, not my friend. So I'd killed her for nothing. She'd been a real friend all the time!'

Her eyes were dilated as she ended her story of horror. Again she was gripping my knees and her sharp nails were biting into my flesh.

'You don't blame me, do you? I'm not a murderess. No one can call me that. It was an accident. An accident. Don't you believe me? Oh God, I can see her face now. Every night in my dreams she stares at me with reproach.'

She covered her face with her hands and sobbed.

'But you won't condemn me, will you?' she appealed, looking up at me. 'I had to do it and it wasn't my fault the two lists got mixed up. It was Fate, Fate – do you hear? You do understand, don't you? I made sure you would understand. Please tell me you understand.'

What was I to do? Give her the reassurance she wanted? Take the load of sin off her chest and let her live the rest of her life in undeserved peace? When all the time my soul cried out against the horror of her deed! No! With a tremendous effort I tore her hands off me and fled from her house, her voice still ringing in my ears. 'You do understand, don't you? I made sure you would understand.'

I had no dinner that night. And I don't go to cocktail parties any more. Suppose I should meet her there? I cannot give her the reassurance she wants and I cannot forget the horrible thing she has done. It was better that we should never meet again – really better so.

But I never stop thinking about her. Why had she chosen me as her confidante whom she hardly knew? Why did she feel so sure I would understand? Or, is it that she had seen something in me which made her feel that placed under the same circumstances I would have done the same thing?

It is a disturbing thought.

Terror of the Curse

'The bride is going to die soon.' The voice was not loud, but there was a sudden lull in the music. I looked towards a group of women under the red canopy but could not discover which of them had spoken. They were a typical Lagos group, colourfully dressed in uniform buba, wrapper and 'flying' headtie – with two or three layers of gold chains and coral beads round their necks and curving over their ample bosoms.

'You see,' the voice continued – it was the sort of half-gloating voice our women use when they spread bad news – I now knew which of them had spoken. She was a young woman, very dark, with very smooth skin, the type that is known as *adumaadan*. Her oval face wore a lively look and the bangles of her wrists jingled like tiny bells as she waved her hands about. 'You see, the bridegroom fell from his mother's back when he was a baby. And they say '– I could hear the ghoulish delight in her voice – 'they say a person like that will have seven wives and they will all die.'

There were excited murmurs from the other women.

'Now, this man, you see ...' the voice continued, but the band suddenly blared forth and the rest was drowned in the noise.

There was a touch on my shoulder and I turned to find the bridegroom behind me. The women had had their backs to the house and had not seen him approaching.

'Did you hear what she said?' he asked and his voice was agitated.

Ayodele and I had been friends from childhood. We first met at a public water pump where we had a fight. It was a jolly good fight – he went home with a swollen eye and I got a bleeding nose – and as most good fights do, ours ended in friendship. So I know him thoroughly. It was unfortunate that he should have such a dread of what he called 'evil forces'. His grandfather was an Ifa priest and from him he had learnt about traditional taboos. He was a Christian and he read his Bible regularly. His fear of demons and sorcerers was no less than his fear of the traditional 'evil forces'.

'Who said?' I temporised, trying to find words to soothe him.

'One of the women. Didn't you hear her?'

'I didn't', I lied.

'She said I fell from my mother's back.'

'Yes?'

'And so my wife's going to die.'

'Nonsense.'

'And six other wives too.'

'More nonsense still. Don't you listen to such stupid talk. I shouldn't worry if I were you. Why, what should kill Aduke? She's the picture of health.'

'Childbirth, for example, or …'

'Or what?'

'Or … or … or T.B.,' he ended lamely.

'Don't you see how silly it all is? Why, there's Aduke coming out with the women of the house. Does she look as if she had T.B? In any case, people don't die of tuberculosis these days.'

Ayodele shook his head. Aduke, a big-boned woman of average height, came out and the guests let out a shout. She was dressed in an expensive damask outfit. Under the huge 'gele' on her head, her large eyes shone with a happiness which in modesty she tried to conceal. She planted a pound note on the forehead of the head drummer, and started dancing; other girls in her age group joined her.

'Where's the bridegroom?' The bride's father asked.

I pushed Ayodele forward and he joined his wife. His male friends followed suit. Soon afterwards he took his bride home.

I gave no further thought to Ayodele's fears till three months later when he rushed into my house looking worried.

'What's the matter?' I asked.

'It's Aduke,' he said.

Terror of the Curse

'Well?'

'I don't know what's wrong with her? I think she's dying.'

'What makes you think so?'

'Well, you see, she's so listless and tires very easily and yesterday she fainted in the kitchen.'

'Has she seen a doctor?' I asked.

'I suggested it and she said it wasn't necessary as she was now all right. I think she's seriously ill and is trying to hide it from me.'

I burst into laughter.

'Silly idiot,' I said, 'your wife is expecting a baby!'

'Do you think so?'

'I am quite certain.'

His face became radiant with pleasure. I plied him with drink and he went home happy and slightly tipsy.

I might have known it wouldn't last. As time went on and Aduke grew bigger, Ayodele began to panic.

'Suppose she were to die?'

I told him thousands of women had babies every year.

'Some of them die.'

'Very few nowadays,' I said, 'and your wife needn't be one of them.'

But he would not be comforted. The night his wife was confined he came to me.

'I couldn't stay at home,' he said and slumped into a chair.

'Suppose they want you – to tell you the news, I mean.'

'I've told them to come for me here.'

I got out some records and played some music.

'Have you had dinner?' I asked.

'I didn't want any,' he said.

I asked my houseboy to bring him some food. He pecked at it until the fork fell to the floor. After that he gave up trying to eat. Each time there was a knock on the door he jumped up. Then he took to pacing up and down the room.

'Look,' I said, and he halted opposite me.

'Sit down.'

He sat down.

'I hope you won't mind my asking, but are you frightfully in love with your wife?'

I had to ask the question for his wife had been obtained for him by his parents and he hadn't seen her till the day before his marriage.

'In love?' he answered, 'certainly not.'

'Then why, ...?' I made a gesture with my pipe.

'It's not Aduke I'm worried about. Can't you see that if she should die it proves the curse is on me? Imagine, one, two, three, seven wives must die before I can be happy. Oh God!'

He put his head on his hands. He was in this attitude when the knock came. Perhaps he did not hear it for he did not move. I opened the door. A little boy nearly fell into the room.

'Is brother Ayo here?' he asked.

'Anything wrong?' I asked.

He looked past me and saw his brother. He went towards him and said, 'Brother, brother, auntie told me to tell you sister has delivered.'

He jumped up at once.

'What is it?' he asked, his eyes boring into the boy's.

'A boy.'

He turned to me excitedly. 'Did you hear what he said? A boy!.'

'So you see ...' I said meaningly. And once again death was averted.

Ayodele seemed to be preoccupied with his child and for a long time I heard no more about the curse.

Then a cholera epidemic broke out in the town. It raged as it had never done before. The hospitals were filled, the *babalawos* were kept busy working charms, and vaccinators were to be seen in Government Health Centres jabbing needles into people. Ayodele was quite convinced that the cholera outbreak had been sent by some malignant fate purposely to slay his wife.

'But, my dear Ayo,' I said, 'Surely that's a bit too much.'

And then he caught it. He sent his wife and the child away

to his parents and his sister stayed on to take care of him. I visited him several times in hospital.

'I hope this has convinced you there's no malignant fate pursuing your wife,' I said.

He gave a sickly smile.

'She hasn't escaped yet. The cholera is still raging.'

Soon he got well, but insisted his wife should stay on with his parents for a little longer. He enjoyed reading his wife's letters even in the semi-literate handwriting. Once, he told me, 'My wife wants to stay on longer with my parents. She says they get on quite well. My parents too say they like her very much. She's so cheerful and everybody likes her. I'm glad she gets on so well with them. It doesn't do to have a wife not liked by one's parents. It brings trouble.'

Once when I visited him he asked me to post a letter for him. I was just going away with it when he asked for it back. He took his pen and, taking the letter out of the envelope, inserted a postcript. I couldn't help seeing it.

'Any cholera in the village yet?' he wrote, then put the letter in another envelope and addressed it.

I smiled and took the letter from him.

One day, he invited me to lunch. I called at his office and we both went to his house. There we found his mother and two other female relatives waiting. There was an air of mourning about them. They sat slumped forward on the mat and greeted us sadly. A little boy gurgled at us from where he sat in front of Ayodele's mother. Filled with apprehension, Ayodele rushed towards them.

'What's wrong?' he asked, his hands shaking.

His mother burst into tears and the two relatives followed suit.

'What is it?' Ayodele repeated. 'Is it about – Aduke?' he gulped.

His mother nodded. 'It's not really our fault. I didn't think there was anything wrong at first and when I knew I didn't dare tell you. We tried our best, your father and I ...'

'Is she dead?' Ayodele asked in despair.

'Dead? No. It's worse. She's run away with a businessman. They're now in London.'

The three women looked at him with anxiety. His mother was shaking her head sorrowfully and the other women were fidgetting with their shawls.

'Is that all, Mother?' Ayodele burst into laughter. He turned to me, 'Let's go and eat,' he said and called out to the houseboy, 'Telemi, make some *amala* for my mothers.'

There was no curse after all.

The Voice by the Lagoon

Izedomi had reached the end. He had thought over his whole life and reached the conclusion that he would be better off dead. He was going to kill himself. 'I am not mad,' he told himself over and over again. Only stupid coroners talked about 'suicide while of an unsound mind.' What did they know about misery? A formula it was to them – just a formula – 'suicide while of an unsound mind.' Why don't they say that when a man murders another? Why do they say it when a man kills himself? A man murdering another destroys his own peace of mind, whereas a man who kills himself gives himself peace at last. "After life's fitful fever, he sleeps well," Izedomi quoted. Well, he was going to give himself the sleep he needed so much – the sleep he had been denied of late. He smiled bitterly as he thought of his defiance of God. Only a few moments ago it was, but it seemed ages ago since he had shouted at God in the anguish of his heart, in the solitude of his room, 'I hate you, God, I hate you! Call yourself God? You are no God but a sadist, delighting in the sufferings of men, in the humiliation of your lowly creatures. Just pawns in your hands to be moved and sacrificed as you please for your personal edification.' He had sneered, 'You want us all to be like Job, don't you?' 'Well, I' – and he had struck his chest forcibly – 'I am not going to be a Job. I defy you. I detest you. Now do your worst!'

He had wallowed in the blasphemy, savouring every abuse on his tongue, and listening with his mind for some sort of response from God, some sort of reaction to reassure him that he had at last been able to wound God in return. What would God do in retaliation? Hurl down his thunderbolt? Izedomi waited at the end of his defiance, waited with a kind of gloating for the approaching martyrdom. But nothing happened. Nothing at all. Only the silence of his room became more oppressive. 'Oh dear, oh dear,' he laughed harshly. 'He doesn't even think me worth a thunderbolt. Too small, too insignificant, not worth the expense and the noise.' He went on laughing for some time and then suddenly stopped. He pressed his hands against his temples and tried to get up. He must open the window, he must get to the window quickly. He rose and took two steps forward – and collapsed.

When he became conscious, the madness had gone. Instead, dull, heavy melancholy descended on him. He felt calm but it was the calm of despair, not the calm of contentment.

Izedomi sat on the floor where he had fallen and thought about his death. It was going to be simple – just a splash and he would be gone for ever. No, not for ever. The third day – or the fourth – he could not remember what he had read in the papers – his bloated body would be found floating on the lagoon. At first the thought did not please him but then he shrugged and thought – it doesn't really matter, does it? And it would be a shame on God who made him in his own image.

He got up from the floor and took up his cap from a hook. He had always been a meticulous person and even though about to die, he would not go out without his cap. Holding the cap in his right hand, he went to the mirror hanging by a nail on the wall, and looked at himself. The mirror showed the whole of his head and the top part of his *agbada*. A slight distortion in the mirror made his face look shorter than it was. It was normally a pleasant round face with the chin rather short but now the sneer on the face distorted it, making the mouth lopsided and the whole face unpleasant. The eyes in particular, held an intense light. They were normally small and the piercing stare now gave them a feverish look.

Izedomi did not seem to be perturbed by what he saw. He put on the cap, adjusting it carefully. Then for no reason at all he stretched his hands before him in the manner of a priest at the altar. For a few moments he stared at the thick, stubby fingers and the short nails. His eyes became dazed. In a short while he seemed to come back to the present and put his

The Voice by the Lagoon

hands down at his sides. He stared round the room – at the shabby furniture that was occasionally stained with fried oil, at the dingy curtains that proclaimed his failure to the outside world, at the wardrobe, her wardrobe, made of cheap wood. Oh, no, he must not think of her, he must not think of her, he did not want to be mad again as he'd been a few moments ago.

A last lingering survey of the room and he was ready to leave. Suddenly just by his window he heard a terrific bang. This brought him up with a start – it was Christmas Eve. He'd forgotten for a short while but that was really what had brought things to a head – his wife dying so near Christmas. But now he no longer believed in Christmas. He no longer believed in Christ. He pushed the door open and went out.

It was a cold, misty harmattan night. The moon shone palely and lacked a definite outline as if someone had sprinkled ashes over its face. But the streets were bright nonetheless. Bright lights shone from every window in the town and fireworks lit up the sky occasionally. Beside the roads children were playing with Bisco flares while the older ones made bangs with knockouts. The adults were sitting on their front verandahs, eating and drinking. A number of people were making their way to church.

But Izedomi did not see all this. His mind was a blank except for the one thought that he must make his way to the lagoon as soon as possible. So unconscious of his surroundings was he that he would have fallen into a large, open drain filled with bubbling scum if a middle-aged woman had not pushed him away very quickly. Her companion, a younger woman, said with disgust, 'He's drunk. Can't even see where he's going.'

Izedomi continued on his way. He had now left his own quarter of the city and the squalid little houses with their rusty iron roofs were giving way to well-kept bungalows with neat, enclosed front gardens. This was what they called the stranger's part of the city. His own district was teeming with the indigenous inhabitants – a conservative lot, yielding to change very slowly. Some of them were very rich traders but they still lived in their family houses while the new houses which they built were let to strangers.

Here in the new district the celebration was more lavish. The bangs were more frequent and radio receivers blared forth the Christmas message from every open window. To Izedomi it was all a confused babble of noise. He pressed his fingers to his ears and quickened his footsteps. The lagoon could not be very far away now.

A group of masked dancing boys, beating empty food tins with sticks for music, tried to ask him for some money but he brushed them aside impatiently and hurried on. His one concern now was to get away from the noise and the bustle. His heart beat began to quicken as he approached the lagoon. He knew he was near it by the fresh breeze which blew across his face. The houses were becoming fewer and the noise was like a distant hum. Suddenly he found himself trying to remember what he had seen as he came through the town. It became imperative that before he plunged himself into the water he should remember what the world was like – not his own world of misery, of pain, of frustration and disappointment, but the world of others – the glittering world of happy people, surely they must be happy to be making so much noise. But try as he could, he could not remember what he had seen. He suddenly panicked. What had they been celebrating ... he could not remember ... they were celebrating something ... something ... And then it came back to him – just Christmas. He felt relieved. They had no real cause to be happy. They were just pretending. Next week it would be all over and they would creep back into their empty kitchens and put their hands into their empty pockets and be just as miserable as he was now. No, he decided with finality, he wouldn't miss anything by drowning himself. With firm steps he turned the corner and came down to the lagoon. Its smooth surface shone palely like a sheet of unpolished silver. And it was calm, calm, calm. For some time he stood looking at it. He wondered if it would be cold because of the harmattan ... it wouldn't matter anyway once he was in. He went towards the bank and was

The Voice by the Lagoon

about to jump in when a voice cut through the quiet of the night air, 'Go on, jump, you coward, jump!' With a shock Izedomi realised he was not alone. Someone was nearby – a woman, judging by the voice. He turned towards the direction of the voice but he could see nothing. The voice came again, full of mockery and contempt, 'Why do you hesitate? Jump. That's what you came all the way for, isn't it? Go ahead, then. Jump!'

But the wish to jump had left him. Instead a kind of curiosity was awakened in him. Who was this woman who did not try to restrain him? Anybody else would have made a grab for him or at least have told him not to jump. In such a case he would surely have jumped but now he did not wish to jump any longer.

As Izedomi peered here and there a figure detached herself from the shrub towards his left. He had thought it was a shadow – there were many shadows in the place. The woman came up to him and said, 'You wanted to end it all, didn't you?' He stared at the dim figure clad in a big *boubou* and wearing a simple headtie. He could hardly see her face. 'You couldn't stand it any more, could you' the woman went on and it was not a question but a statement. He did not say anything. 'Did you by any chance imagine people would be sorry for you when they heard?' She laughed derisively. 'The world, I can assure you, has no sympathy for failures. They'd have laughed and said, "poor fool". Would you have liked that for an epitaph? Or were you trying to spite someone, to make them guilty that they'd driven you to it?'

He found his tongue at last. 'I wasn't trying to spite anyone. I was just fed up with life.' He did not know why he was explaining to her, but somehow he felt he had to make her understand. To make her realize how a man could be driven to the decision that he could never make good and it was no use. He was wondering how to tell her – her attitude was so forbidding. To his surprise he heard her say in a gentle, kind voice, 'Tell me all about it; it does help to tell someone. It's bottling it up that does the harm.' She came to him and took his arm, leading him to a concrete bench. And as if he had known her all his life, he began to pour out his heart to her.

'You see, both my parents died in a car accident when I was only four and I was brought up by an uncle. His wife was most cruel to me ...' He told her of his sufferings as a child, of having to work on the farm before school, of being caned for coming late to class, of being flogged and sent home for school fees at the beginning of every term, of the jeers of the other children at his patched uniform ...

'And when I grew up it was no better,' he continued. 'It seemed a malicious fate was pursuing me all the time. First, I could not get a job for a long time – you know how it is, if you're not well-connected in this country you don't get anything. Then when I got a job things were no better. In the office I was unhappy. There was nothing I could do right; the boss always railed at me. He knew I had no connections. I wrote petitions to the authorities, but I got no reply. They were all his friends.

'And then I got married to a very sweet girl. She was only nineteen when we married a year ago. If I was bullied in the office I came home to a soothing welcome. I found I was not minding the office so much.' He paused and there was a sob in his voice as he added, 'She died in childbirth three months ago. There was a complication and the hospital had no equipment to deal with it.'

'And the baby?'

'He did not live.'

'And yesterday – two days before Christmas – I got sacked from my job. They did not tell me what I had done. Only said they didn't need my services any more.' He smiled ruefully, 'Any wonder I decided to end it all? After all, I'm completely useless in the world, as you can see. No use to myself, no use to anybody else. No one will miss me, I tell you. I wish you'd let me jump.' The woman did not say anything. He continued, 'I know you told me to jump but that was a sure way of stopping me from jumping.'

The woman said, 'Thank goodness you did not jump.' After

The Voice by the Lagoon

a moment's silence she said. 'Come home with me, at least for Christmas. You cannot stay by yourself.' She got up and he got up too. She led him back the way he had come. He noticed that she walked stiffly and rather slowly. But the distance was not much. After about two hundred metres she turned into a cul-de-sac. At the end of the alley was a bungalow with a large open space in front of it enclosed by a pitanga hedge. Two tarpaulin canopies had been erected in the open space. The security lights were on and the woman went under the porch light and fumbled in her bag. She took out a bunch of keys and opened the door. 'Please come in,' she said, and led the way into the house. She seated him on a settee in the sitting-cum-dining room, a plainly but tastefully furnished room.

'Would you like some tea or do you prefer soft drinks?' she asked him.

Suddenly he felt thirsty. 'A soft drink, please,' he said.

She went to the refridgerator and brought out two bottles, a packet of biscuits and some cake. From the sideboard she brought out two glasses and two side plates. She placed a plate of biscuits and cake, and a glass of soft drink on a stool by the settee. Her movements were very stiff, he noticed. What was the matter with her legs, he wondered. She took her own plate of refreshments to a stool beside an upright cane chair opposite him and sat on the chair. Now that he could see her face clearly he found it a very pleasant face, if a little plump. She had a very warm smile. She was in her late thirties, he guessed. Like him. Her *boubou*, he noticed, covered an ample body. She began to tell him about the Christmas party she was giving for a group of children the next day. He was not really listening to her as he kept on wondering who she was, what she did for a living, and what she had been doing by the lagoon. But he began to pay attention when she said, 'I'd like to ask you a favour. I need someone to take the place of our regular Father Christmas. He's in hospital. Could you help?'

Izedomi remembered his grudge against God. He no longer believed in God and Christmas, so why should be play Father

Christmas to a bunch of kids he'd never seen before in his life? In any case Christmas was a foreign festival. The whole idea of Father Christmas was foreign, anyway, and the costume was ridiculous in the tropical heat. He said to her, 'I am allergic to wool.'

The woman said, 'The costume has no wool. We use cotton for the beard and the trimmings and the material is also cotton.'

He felt he had to tell her. 'I have stopped believing in God and Christmas.'

'Sleep over it,' she said as she got up. 'I'll go and prepare your room.' Later she showed him to his room. Like the sitting-cum-dining room, it was simply furnished, with a single bed, a dressing table and an armchair. On the armchair was a Father Christmas costume and on the bed was a neatly folded nightshirt, obviously one of hers. A bulging red canvas bag trimmed with white leaned against a corner.

Alone in the room, Izedomi sat on the bed. He felt rather resentful towards his hostess. Suppose she hadn't found him, wouldn't she have found someone else to play Father Christmas? Must he play Father Christmas just because she saved his life? The whole thing was meaningless anyway. Religion had become a commercial thing with all sorts of churches and false prophets springing up at every street corner. And yet corruption was escalating every day in the country. The more the churches, the more the prophets, the more the so-called born-again Christians, the more the moral degradation in the country. A God who allowed such things did not deserve to be worshipped. A sudden thought struck him. He had tried to be a good person all his life and yet God had kept on striking him down with blows. Now he would get his own back. He would strike a blow against God. He would play Father Christmas with a vengeance. He would wear the costume quite all right. He would carry the bag of toys over his shoulder. He would go before the children. And then – glorious thought – he would remove his hood and beard. He would reveal himself and tell the children the whole thing was

The Voice by the Lagoon

a sham, a hoax. Izedomi felt cheerful and having arrived at this delightful plan of revenge, he undressed, did not bother with the nightshirt, and stretched himself on the bed. He never wore anything in bed, anyway.

He must have been very tired from his emotional exertions for he did not wake until nine the next morning. He got up, had a bath and put on his clothes. Then he went into the sitting-cum-dining room.

He could hear his hostess in the kitchen and wondered if he should go there and say good morning to her, but before he could do so she came in with a tray of breakfast things. She stopped when she saw him and said, 'You're up at last. I can see you slept well.' She smiled and put the tray on the dining table which was already laid for two. Then she looked at him questioningly, 'Have you decided?'

Izedomi smiled and asked, 'What time is the party?'

'Two o'clock. Will you …?'

'Yes, of course.'

She heaved a sigh of relief and Izedomi felt rather guilty. If only she knew what he had planned. But he had to do it. Since she would not let him kill himself, she was also in conspiracy with God and deserved whatever she got.

Breakfast was fried bean balls – *akara* – and boiled millet meal eaten with sugar and milk. The *akara* was fluffy and tasty with just enough pepper and onion to give it a little spicy tang. 'She is a good cook,' Izedomi thought as he helped himself to the cakes. After breakfast, he said, 'I'd like to go for a stroll,' and she looked anxious again.

'Don't worry, I'll be back. I don't want to miss the party. Not for anything in the world. I've never played Father Christmas before.'

The woman thought what a change a good night's sleep could work on the mind. She went to the backyard where the catering for the party was being done on open wood fires in huge three-legged iron pots by some women helpers.

Izedomi came back from his stroll at noon and saw that the party arena had been decorated with colourful balloons, streamers, bunting and Christmas decorations. It looked very festive. A bandstand had been erected at one end and musical instruments placed on it. A technician was testing a microphone by blowing into it and shouting. 'Testing, testing, testing.'

Izedomi had told his hostess that since *akara* was so filling, he would not attend the first half of the party. He was afraid he might not be able to carry out his revenge if he started feasting with the children. As soon as he had carried out his exposure he would leave. So he picked up a book from the bookshelf in the sitting-dining room and went into his bedroom, shutting the door to keep out the sound of merriment. But his mind was not on the book he was reading. He kept on rehearsing what he would say to the children. When the woman came for him he had not quite decided in what words he would carry out the exposure. He put on his costume, slung the heavy bundle of toys over his shoulder and followed his hostess out.

Izedomi was shocked by the sight that met his eyes. About fifty children of various ages and with all kinds of handicaps were seated under the canopies. Some were on wheel chairs. His hostess, dressed in a beautifully embroidered red brocade *boubou* with a red and silver headtie, announced, 'Now, children, Father Christmas is here. He's going to give you presents.'

Excited cries greeted this announcement. The children soon quietened down and looked at him expectantly. His hostess moved aside and motioned him forward. For a moment he hesitated, then stepped forward and put his bag down. He opened it and took out the first present. Shrill cries of delight greeted each parcel and Izedomi found his heart warming to the children. A happy glow suffused his whole being. He experienced for the first time in his life the joy of giving. He forgot that the gifts were not his originally, he forgot his own unhappiness and thought only of the delight he was giving these unfortunate yet fortunate children. A gospel band played as the distribution went on. When he finished giving out the gifts, he sat down beside his hostess. After the children had all gone, Izedomi said to his hostess, 'I think you owe me an explanation, and I think you ought to tell me your name. Mine is Izedomi Oraaga.'

The woman said. 'I'm called Okanima,' 'Okanima Aimakhu.'

Izedomi was surprised. 'We come from the same state,' he exclaimed.

'It's a small world,' she said, smiling.

'Those children – where were they from?' Izedomi asked. 'What's your connection with them?'

'Let's go into the house.' She got up and they went into the sitting/dining room. They both sat on the settee.

'The explanation,' Izedomi prompted.

Okanima sighed wistfully and began, 'One of those children saved my life once. Olohigbe, she's called. You know the meaning?'

'Of course. She who is not destined to die …'

'I gave her the name and I think it's very appropriate. She saved my life and I saved her life.'

'What happened?'

'You see, I was in despair when I first saw her, near some mangrove trees by the lagoon. I was going to drown myself because life had become meaningless to me. I come from a very rich family and had always had everything I wanted. I had a lot of suitors in those days and after some time I got engaged to a very handsome young man who also came from a good family. Everything was fine for me until one day a car knocked me down as I was crossing a road. There was a long line of stationary cars before a railway crossing. I was on the other side of the road and no car was coming. Suddenly an army jeep started overtaking all the stationary cars. I did not see it because I was not expecting it and it moved very fast. It knocked me down. My right leg was crushed and had to be amputated. I was in hospital for months, but my fiance only came to see me once. When I came out he had gone overseas. My other suitors too had disappeared. None of them wanted a cripple on their hands. And so one lonely Christmas Eve I came to the same conclusion as you came to last night. I made my way to the lagoon but just as I was about to jump in I heard a cry. It was a baby's cry. When I went to see I found she was about three month's old. Her legs were twisted in an unnatural way. It was obvious she would never walk. I took her to the police station and asked if I could keep her until they found the parents. They never did. So I sent her to the motherless babies' home and paid for her keep. Later I had her transferred to a home for the handicapped. Since then I have supported children in a number of homes. I derive great pleasure from giving happiness and security to these children.'

'Luckily, you have the money to do it with,' Izedomi said.

'Money is not everything. The children need love and understanding too. They need to live normal or near-normal lives, take part in social activities, develop their talents, that kind of thing. We need helpers. By 'we' I mean the association for the physically handicapped. I am the president.'

She turned to him, 'Were you ever a boy scout?'

'Yes,' Izedomi said, 'and I worked in the social welfare department before I was laid off.'

'We can't pay much but I would appreciate your coming to work for us.'

She looked at him hopefully.

'I'd love to,' Izedomi said.

'So you see your life is of use after all.'

'I agree. But tell me, why did you go to the lagoon on Christmas Eve?'

'Shall we say, I went to look for Father Christmas.'

She patted his hand and they both smiled at each other.

GLOSSARY

abiku
a child who keeps on dying and being reincarnated again and again in the same woman

acada
short for *academician*, an intellectual university graduate

adumaadan
endearment term for a girl or woman with a very smooth black skin, 'black and shining woman'

agbada
a loose outer garment worn by men

akara
fried bean balls

amala
yam flour stirred in boiling water until it becomes doughy

apu
cooked fermented, pounded cassava

ayo
a traditional game played with seeds in a wooden tray with twelve 'rooms' or compartments

babalawo
traditional healer

boubou
women's loose, ankle-length dress, originally worn by Guinean and Senegalese women

buba
loose blouse with a square cut worn by women with wrappers (cloth wrapped around the waist)

chop
pidgin English (originally spoken by domestic servants in colonial days but now widespread) for *eat*. To *eat* money in Yoruba means 'to embezzle money or to convert other people's money to one's own use'

eba
starchy food made from grated, fermented roasted cassava (gari)

eko
cooked corn meal wrapped in leaves and cooled or made into hot porridge

e ku 'le
a Yoruba greeting said to people who have remained at home while the speaker was out. The Yoruba who live in the south-west part of Nigeria have a greeting for every occasion

e wole
come in

foofoo
thick boiled starch eaten with a stew

Fulani
an ethnic group found in the north-east of the country

gari
grated, fermented roasted cassava

gele
women's headtie

Ibo
an ethnic group found in the eastern part of the country

Ifa
oracle invoked by the priests of a Yoruba traditional religious sect

Ikoyi
an exclusive part of Lagos

juju
object venerated in West Africa as a charm or fetish; a supernatural power attributed to this

kickback
money given to an official as bribe for awarding a contract to the giver

Glossary

kolanuts
bitter seeds chewed by people in the same way as people use cigarettes; it is also used in traditional ceremonies

molue
a type of bus that plies Lagos roads

naira
currency used in Nigeria

ogogoro
local gin made from palm wine

orogbo
bitter kolanuts

pitanga
a hedge plant with dark berries

tokunbo
literally '(he or she) who came from overseas' a name usually given to a child born overseas

waka
a swear word usually accompanied by a rude gesture

Also in Longman African Writers

The Stillborn

Zaynab Alkali

The Stillborn is a moving and inspiring first novel which places Zaynab Alkali among that select group of writers who have focused and deepened our understanding of the situation of women in the African continent.

BBC, WORLD SERVICE

Zaynab Alkali, one of the first women novelists of Northern Nigeria, centres her first novel around the experiences of women in contemporary Nigeria. *The Stillborn* follows the adolescent plans and dreams of Li – as she struggles for independence against the traditional values of the family home, marriage and the lure of the city and all that can offer. In the final scenes of the novel a mature, confident yet more tolerant Li chooses the city and a chance to establish a life on her own terms.

ISBN 0 582 26432 4

The Beggars Strike

Aminata Sow Fall

The sight of disease-ridden beggars in the streets is giving the town a bad name, and the tourists are starting to stay away. If the Director of Public Health and Hygiene can get rid of them he will have done a great service to the health and economy of the nation – not to mention his own promotional prospects. A plan of military precision is put into action to rid the streets of these verminous scroungers.

But the beggars are organised, too.

They know that giving alms is a divine obligation and that Allah's goodwill is vital to worldly promotion. So when the beggars withdraw their charitable service the pious city civil servants and businessmen start to panic.

This brilliant satire on conflicting values in the pushy world of the developing African city won the 1980 Grand Prix de Littérature de l'Afrique Noire and was short-listed for France's prestigious Prix Goncourt.

Clear sighted writing around a neat and extraordinary plot.

SPARE RIB

a delicious satirical fable

TIMES EDUCATIONAL SUPPLEMENT

ISBN 0 582 00243 5

Scarlet Song

Mariama Ba

Translated by Dorothy S. Blair

Mariama Ba's first novel *So Long a Letter* was the winner of the Noma Award in 1980. In this her second and, tragically, last novel she displays all the same virtues of warmth and crusading zeal for women's rights that won her so many admirers for her earlier work.

Mireille, daughter of a French diplomat and Ousmane, son of a poor Muslim family in Senegal, are two childhood sweethearts forced to share their love in secret. Their marriage shocks and dismays both sets of parents, but it soon becomes clear that their youthful optimism and love offer a poor defence against the pressures of society. As Ousmane is lured back to his roots, Mireille is left humiliated, isolated and alone.

The tyranny of tradition and chauvinism is brilliantly exposed in this passionate plea for human understanding. The author's sympathetic insights into the condition of women deserve recognition throughout the world.

ISBN 0 582 78595 2

Between Two Worlds

Miriam Tlali

Banned when it was first published in South Africa *Between Two Worlds* (formerly *Muriel at Metropolitan*) is one of the most distinctive novels to have come out of South Africa. The tale is set in a bustling furniture and electronics store catering for poor whites and blacks. It describes the daily experiences of the black accounts typist, Muriel, her relationships with her colleagues and her feelings about the stream of customers who come into the shop. It is remarkable for its combination of gentle humour and wealth of detail about life on the fringes of white society. Miriam Tlali's first novel gives evidence of a rare and precious talent.

Ought to be compulsory reading. It's humourous, witty and clearly written: the injustice and tragedy are no less plain for being unpolemically shown.

THE ENGLISH MAGAZINE

Transparently honest. What must have been a strong temptation to sensationalise events is firmly resisted.

WEST AFRICA

ISBN 0 582 01657 6

Other Titles Available

Longman African Writers

Title	Author	ISBN
A Forest of Flowers	K Saro-Wiwa	0 582 27320 X
Sozaboy	K Saro-Wiwa	0 582 23699 1
Tides	I Okpewho	0 582 10276 6
Of Men and Ghosts	K Aidoo	0 582 22871 9
Flowers and Shadows	B Okri	0 582 03536 8
The Victims	I Okpewho	0 582 26502 9
Call Me Not a Man	M Matshoba	0 582 00242 7
Dilemma Of a Ghost/Anowa	A A Aidoo	0 582 27602 0
Our Sister Killjoy	A A Aidoo	0 582 00391 1
No Sweetness Here	A A Aidoo	0 582 26456 1
The Marriage of Anansewa/ Edufa	E Sutherland	0 582 00245 1
Children of Soweto	M Mzamane	0 582 26434 0
The Life of Olaudah Equiano	P Edwards	0 582 26473 1
Sundiata	D T Niane	0 582 26475 8
The Last Duty	I Okpewho	0 582 78535 9
Hungry Flame	M Mzamane	0 582 78590 1
Fools	N Ndebele	0 582 78621 5
Master and Servant	D Mulwa	0 582 78632 0
The Park	J Matthews	0 582 26435 9
Sugarcane With Salt	James Ng'ombe	0 582 05204 1

Other Titles Available

Longman Caribbean Writers

Caribbean New Voices	S Brown (Ed)	0 582 23702 8
Consolation	E G Long	0 582 23913 3
Between Two Seasons	I J Boodhoo	0 582 22869 7
Satellite City	A McKenzie	0 582 08688 4
Karl and other stories	V Pollard	0 582 22726 7
Homestretch	V Pollard	0 582 22732 1
Discoveries	J Wickham	0 582 21804 7
Chieftain's Carnival	M Anthony	0 582 21805 5
DreamStories	E Braithwaite	0 582 09340 6
Arrival of the Snakewoman	O Senior	0 582 03170 2
Summer Lightning	O Senior	0 582 78627 4
The Dragon Can't Dance	E Lovelace	0 582 64231 0
Ways of Sunlight	S Selvon	0 582 64261 2
The Lonely Londoners	S Selvon	0 582 64264 7
A Brighter Sun	S Selvon	0 582 64265 5
Foreday Morning	S Selvon	0 582 03982 7
In the Castle of my Skin	G Lamming	0 582 64267 1
My Bones and My Flute	E Mittelholzer	0 582 78552 9
Black Albino	N Roy	0 582 78563 4
The Children of Sisyphus	O Patterson	0 582 78571 5
The Jumbie Bird	I Khan	0 582 78619 3
Study Guide to The Jumbie Bird	S G-Maharaj	0 582 25652 6
Plays for Today	E Hill et al	0 582 78620 7
Old Story Time and Smile Orange	T D Rhone	0 582 78633 9
Study Guide to Old Story Time	M Morris	0 582 23703 3
Baby Mother and the King of Swords	L Goodison	0 582 05492 3
Two Roads to Mount Joyful	E McKenzie	0 582 07125 9
Voiceprint	S Brown et al	0 582 78629 0

These titles can be obtained or ordered from your local bookseller. For further information on titles and study guides available contact your local Longman agent or Longman International Education, Longman Group Limited, Longman House, Burnt Mill, Harlow, Essex, CM20 2JE, England.